The plan was just too risky....

"I still think it would be better if I did this alone," he said. "If something happens to me, you'll still be alive and able to figure another way out of this."

"You need someone to watch your back, otherwise it's just a suicide mission." Her gaze sharpened. "And at least one of us cares whether you live or die."

He recognized that stubborn gleam in her eye. Arguing would just be wasting breath.

Audrey suddenly got quiet. "Even if the plan works, it seems wrong that the truth won't come out."

"All I care about is you not being killed."

Only when the words were out did he consider how they might have come across. Like she mattered to him. Which she did, he immediately recognized, his chest tightening.

He didn't want it to be the case, and he'd done his best to fight it. But suddenly he knew the thought of anything happening to Audrey scared the hell out of him.

KERRY CONNOR

CIRCUMSTANTIAL MARRIAGE

TORONTO NEW YORK LONDON
AMSTERDAM PARIS SYDNEY HAMBURG
STOCKHOLM ATHENS TOKYO MILAN MADRID
PRAGUE WARSAW BUDAPEST AUCKLAND

To Patty, my favorite journalist and an even better friend.

ISBN-13: 978-0-373-69535-5

Recycling programs for this product may not exist in your area.

CIRCUMSTANTIAL MARRIAGE

ABOUT THE AUTHOR

A lifelong mystery reader, Kerry Connor first discovered romantic suspense by reading Harlequin Intrigue books and is thrilled to be writing for the line. Kerry lives and writes in New York.

Books by Kerry Connor

HARLEQUIN INTRIGUE

Don't miss any of our special offers. Write to us at the following address for information on our newest releases.

Harlequin Reader Service
U.S.: 3010 Walden Ave., P.O. Box 1325, Buffalo, NY 14269
Canadian: P.O. Box 609, Fort Erie, Ont. L2A 5X3

CAST OF CHARACTERS

Audrey Ellison—She was targeted for death by forces determined to keep a long-hidden secret from being revealed.

Jason Stone—A man who'd lost everything, he had no interest in anyone else's secrets, but he couldn't stand by when a woman running for her life came to him for help.

Hal Talmadge—The journalist had uncovered the scoop of a lifetime—one that cost him his life.

Richard Bridges—A politician with a bright future...and a dark secret in his past?

Dick Bridges—Seeing his son become president was his life's ambition. How far would he go to see it fulfilled?

Julia Bridges—Was the ideal political wife as perfect as she seemed?

Marybeth Kent—The innkeeper wasn't a fan of her hometown's favorite son.

Will Kent—The small-town mayor had big-time aspirations of his own.

Tim Raymer—A name from the past that kept coming up.

Clint Raymer—He had plenty to say, but could he be believed?

Albert Shaw—A man with a job to do and no qualms about doing it.

Prologue

In the two years Audrey Ellison had lived in her apartment building, she had never felt unsafe there. Living in a big city like Baltimore, she knew to be careful and alert to her surroundings, but her neighborhood was decent and the quiet four-story brownstone had never been anything but peaceful. So, as she climbed the stairs to her third-floor apartment at one that morning, she had no reason to feel uneasy.

Instead, she simply felt exhausted, barely capable of making it up the stairs. She never stayed out this late on a weeknight, but her friend Jackie was getting married over the weekend, and Audrey had been roped into one last, impromptu girls' night out to celebrate Jackie's impending nuptials and final days as a single woman. Audrey hadn't intended to stay as long as she had, but had gotten caught up in the festivities and lost track of the time.

Jackie hadn't stopped beaming once all night, Audrey thought with a smile of her own. Getting to share in Jackie's happiness was worth the lost sleep that would inevitably leave her dragging in the morning. If she was honest, it gave her hope that happy endings still existed, and someday she herself might find what Jackie and so many of her friends had. Someday....

She finally reached the third-floor landing. The smile still on her face, she unlocked and opened her door, thinking only of stumbling to her bedroom and collapsing into bed.

Stepping inside, she kicked the door shut behind her without turning on the light. She didn't plan to be in the living room long enough to need it. Reaching for the strap of her messenger bag to lift it over her head, she started to ease out of her shoes.

The prickle of unease at the back of her neck was her only warning. It came out of nowhere, pure animal instinct. The sensation snapped her awake and made her go still.

Her eyes flicked over the darkened room, the faint light that managed to break through the curtains offering little illumination. She could see nothing, hear nothing. She knew just the same.

Something was wrong.

She dropped the strap of her bag and reached out to turn the light on after all.

She never got the chance.

Two seconds later something hard and round pressed against the back of her skull.

She froze, even before a low, deep voice ordered, "Don't move."

That vague sense of unease exploded into full-fledged terror at both the man's presence and the instinctive knowledge of what he was pushing into her head.

It was a gun. There was a man in her apartment with a gun pointed at her head.

It didn't seem real. Who was he? How had he gotten into her apartment? What did he want?

The only question asked aloud came from him. "Audrey Ellison?"

Her pulse leaped at the sound of her name. He knew who she was. That erased any possibility this was just a case of mistaken identity or a simple burglary. He'd been waiting for her in the dark.

She didn't know what to say. If she admitted it, would he pull the trigger? If she denied it, would he do the same, getting her out of the way to wait for the "real" Audrey?

"Answer me," he ordered.

The cold hardness of the demand shocked her into responding without thinking. "Yes," she whispered, the word loud in the stillness. She braced herself for his reaction.

"Do you have a copy of the book?"

She blinked into the darkness, not understanding. The words didn't make any sense. "What book?" she made herself say.

"The book your uncle was working on."

Clarity came in a burst. She had only one uncle, only one living relative, in fact. Hal was an award-winning journalist. His current top secret project was a biography of Senator Richard Bridges, the popular politician who was about to officially announce his run for the presidency, something, by all indications, he would win. Hal had been working on the book for almost a year and was on the verge of finishing. She knew he was excited about it, was convinced it was going to be all anyone was talking about upon its release. He said the book was going to be his legacy. On the few occasions she'd spoken to him over the past year, he'd made it clear he thought he'd found something juicy about the squeaky-clean Bridges.

Which he must have, she realized. The only reason this man could be here, the only reason he could be asking about the book, was if Hal had found something. Something Bridges didn't want to get out. *Bridges must have sent this man.*

But why come to her? Why not—

The man's exact words finally sank in. *Was* working on. That was what the man had said. Was. Past tense. He didn't think Hal was working on it anymore.

Her breath caught in her throat. Oh, God. Had something happened to Hal?

The man drove the barrel of the gun harder into her skin, the pain making her wince. "Do you have a copy?" he repeated, emphasizing each word, his impatience clear.

Still, she hesitated. What should she say? She didn't have a copy, of course. Hal was so secretive about his work, she would bet anything he was the only one who'd seen the book or had any idea what was in it. She'd been surprised he'd revealed as much about it to her as he had. But if she told the truth, would the man just shoot her?

She needed a plan. She needed an escape.

Her fingers tightened on the keys still clutched in her right hand. As soon as she felt what was there, she had her answer.

Another jab of the gun. "Well?"

"No," she said slowly.

He didn't say anything for a moment. Was he trying to decide if she was telling the truth?

"Did your uncle tell you what was in it?"

"No. He wouldn't tell anyone. Hal is always so secretive about his work. He keeps everything close until he's ready to reveal it to the world." Audrey knew she was babbling, hoped it covered any sound she was making in her hand until she had the object she wanted.

There was another interminable silence. Then the man finally said, "You wouldn't be lying to me, would you? Because if you are…"

She didn't wait to find out the ending to that sentence. She simultaneously ducked her head and raised her hand, sending pepper spray shooting behind her from the small canister clipped to her key ring. The low roar that met her ears told her she'd hit her target. She lunged for the door, jerking it open and plunging into the hall. There was a rush of air against her back—his hands reaching for her, or a bullet?—but nothing stopped her as she lurched toward the stairs.

She didn't look behind her as she dashed down them, moving so quickly she almost tripped and stumbled. She didn't let herself, couldn't miss a step, couldn't fall. She had to get away. She had to get out of here. She had to get help.

She made it to one landing, then the next. She waited for an angry shout, for the sound of footsteps behind her, for the impact of a bullet. They never came. Almost before she knew it, she reached the front doors and was crashing through them.

Still she didn't stop. She'd parked halfway down the block in a space on the street. When she was midway there, she finally risked a glance back. No one came out of the building, no one was on the street paying her any attention. The fact did nothing to ease her tension. The man didn't have to be alone. There could be someone else, waiting in a car, waiting to ambush her now.

The idea made her pick up speed. She finally made it to the car, throwing herself into the driver's seat and slamming the locks shut.

Only when she was peeling out of the parking space did she consider where to go now. She knew getting away had only temporarily solved her problem. Even if they believed she hadn't seen the book and didn't know what was in it, the fact that she now knew that there was something Bridges wanted hidden meant she was still a target, maybe even more of one than before.

Audrey checked her mirrors, trying to see if anyone was following. It didn't look like it, but that fact didn't make her feel any better. She clamped her hands on the steering wheel and pressed down on the accelerator, wanting to put as much distance as possible between her and the man in her apartment.

She knew immediately she couldn't go to the police. Richard Bridges was a United States senator. The front-runner to be the next president of the United States before he even officially announced his candidacy. The man had to have connections everywhere. He'd somehow managed to find out that Hal had uncovered something about him before Hal told anyone else or turned in the book.

Hal.

Her thoughts screeched to a halt. Fumbling in her

bag with one hand, she pulled out her phone. Maybe she was wrong. Maybe he was fine. Maybe…

She hit the speed dial for Hal's home number and waited as the line rang, her heart climbing into her throat with every subsequent buzz.

No answer.

She automatically redialed, turning the car toward D.C. She had to go to Hal's house. He could be asleep. He could have the ringer off. She clung to the slight hope the ideas offered. He could be fine. And if he was, he would know what was going on. Either way, she had to go to D.C.

One hour later, she sat on Hal's street, staring down the block toward Hal's town house.

Or at least, where Hal's town house had been.

There was nothing there now but the charred husk of a burnt-out structure. Crime scene tape blocked off the front of the space, fluttering slightly in the night wind. There were no fire engines or police vehicles in view, nor could she see any investigators poking through the rubble. The street was quiet. The fire must have happened hours ago, long enough for peace to settle in again.

No.

The word pressed at her lips, nearly emerging as a sob. The burnt building before her began to swim as tears filled her eyes. She made no move to wipe them away, unable to do anything but sit there, hands on the wheel, and stare at the horrible sight in front of her.

The man in her apartment had been telling the truth. She had no doubt that Hal had been inside the building when it went up in flames.

Hal was dead.

He hadn't been much of an uncle, always too consumed by his career to give a thought to his only niece. If she hadn't made the effort to give him a call every now and then, she doubted he would have bothered keeping in touch himself. But he'd been all she had, ever since the deaths of her parents when she was eleven.

And now he was gone.

The sob finally slipped free, the watery sound of it filling the car's interior. She felt the tears pouring down her face and swiped at them. She couldn't do this. Not now. There wasn't time. She shot a frantic glance around her to make sure no one was watching or had noticed her sitting here. Reassured when she didn't spot anyone, she put the car into gear, sniffling back the last of the tears.

She had to get out of here. She had to find someone who could help her, someone she could trust.

As the car raced away from Hal's street, her mind remained stubbornly blank. She certainly didn't have those kinds of connections anymore. She was a family photographer. She took pictures at weddings, of schoolchildren. Family portraits. She hadn't kept in touch with anyone from her own reporter days. Even if she knew how to contact someone, she couldn't trust them with this.

Hal would have, of course. He knew people. He would have known what to do, and if he hadn't, then one of his connections would.

Unless one of them had betrayed him.

Frustration and fear churned inside her. She had to

find out what had happened to Hal. And she had to figure out where to go. Somewhere they wouldn't find her.

Jason Stone.

The name floated to the forefront of her mind out of nowhere, and as soon as it appeared, everything inside her went still, certainty taking hold within her.

Of course. There was one person she could trust.

Jason Stone.

He'd been Hal's protégé, a promising young reporter who'd gone on to be a highly acclaimed journalist in his own right. If there was one person Hal would have talked to about the book, it was him. He was one of the few people Hal respected and trusted, and if she remembered correctly, he'd covered Richard Bridges early in his career. Not to mention, Hal wouldn't have considered him a professional rival.

Because Jason Stone wasn't a reporter anymore. Two years ago, he'd quit his job and left every remnant of his former life behind. According to Hal, he'd deliberately disappeared, doing his best to ensure no one could find him. Still, she had the feeling Hal was one of the few people—perhaps the only one—who knew where Stone was. If Stone hadn't told him, Hal would have found him, especially once he started working on the book about a subject Stone was familiar with. Everyone knew how close Hal and Stone had been.

Which meant anyone looking for someone Hal would have talked to about the book would be looking for him, too.

A jolt shot through her. She slammed her foot down on the accelerator, adrenaline and determination surging through her veins. She couldn't continue using her phone, couldn't risk her location being tracked. She had to find an internet café, had to get started on tracking down Stone immediately. He was the only person she could think of who could help her, and if she was right, the only person in as much danger as she was.

She had to find him first, for Hal's sake and their own.

Both their lives depended on it.

Chapter One

It was no place for a lady.

That was how Jason Stone's elderly neighbor had described the bar where she said he was most likely to be if he wasn't home. Now that she was here, Audrey could see the woman's description had been too generous.

This was no place for anyone.

A thin cloud of smoke hung over the room, obscuring the already dim lighting behind a white haze. From what she could tell, the furnishings were old and dingy. A few ancient beer signs flickered uncertainly on the walls, casting an eerie glow. Other than the clink of glasses being raised and set down again and some voices lowered ominously in muffled conversation, the room was unnervingly silent. There wasn't even a TV or radio turned on to fill the quiet.

Under normal circumstances, Audrey wouldn't dream of stepping foot in a seedy dive in one of D.C.'s roughest neighborhoods. But the circumstances were anything but normal, and the regular rules didn't apply. After three days of living out of her car, sneaking computer time at public libraries and internet cafés while searching for a man who no longer seemed to exist, she wasn't going to turn back now.

Instead, she ignored the forbidding atmosphere and ducked through the doorway into the bar. A twinge of relief passed through her as soon as she stepped out of the sunlight. She couldn't afford to stay outside any longer. She was too exposed out in the open. They might find her. Then all the effort she'd put into finding Stone would be for nothing.

It hadn't been easy. Jason Stone had done everything he could to avoid being found. He had no known address. His phone number wasn't listed anywhere, if he even had one. A credit check had revealed no activity: no credit cards, no bank accounts, no outstanding loans. Two years ago he'd sold his house, quit his job and virtually disappeared, leaving no trace to his whereabouts. He could have gone anywhere in the world by now.

She'd managed to track him down just the same.

She had no doubt he wouldn't be happy about it. A man didn't go to such lengths if he wanted to be found.

Too bad she hadn't had a choice.

Now the trail led here. Pulling her long coat tighter around herself, Audrey narrowed her eyes and scanned the faces of the assembled bar patrons for the one she sought. She'd never met the man before, only seen pictures of him. It was hard to imagine the dashing figure from those images in a place like this, but then, a lot could happen in two years.

The heels of her boots clacked loudly against the hardwood floor, the sound echoing in the enclosed space. Not for the first time in the past few days, she wished she had different shoes. But that was just one of the problems of having limited funds and being unable to go back to her apartment. She didn't exactly have a lot of wardrobe options left to her. She cringed at the noise, fully expecting people to turn and stare. None of the patrons so much as glanced in her direction, keeping their heads bowed and their attention on their drinks. Only the bartender watched her. His hooded gaze slid slowly up and down her body with a level of focus that made her skin crawl. Repressing a shudder, Audrey looked away. She might have asked him if he knew Stone, but she had the feeling the information would cost her more than she was willing to give.

None of the faces jumped out at first glance as the one she sought. She walked slowly, giving each a second look, then a third. Her stomach knotted painfully with each one she dismissed. A growing sense of unease clawed at her insides and she swallowed hard. He had to be here. If he wasn't, her only choice would be to go back and wait at his building for his return, and if she'd been able to find out where he lived, they could, too.

If they hadn't already.

Fighting a wave of hopelessness, she was about to turn around and risk asking the bartender when something drew her back toward a man hunched over a table in the back of the room. She'd glanced past him three times, nothing about him striking an immediate chord. Still, something in the back of her mind prodded her to look closer. It wasn't easy. But as she peered through the gloom, something clicked into place and she realized the solitary figure nursing a beer was the man she sought.

Shock held her relief at bay. She froze, momentarily

stunned. He was wearing a threadbare sweater and, rather oddly for the indoor setting, leather gloves. He had shaggy, shoulder-length brown hair, a far cry from the perfectly groomed man in his pictures. His head was bowed, the long hair nearly managing to cover his face. Enough of his strong profile emerged from behind that dark brown curtain to reveal his identity, once she looked close enough.

This was Jason Stone. Her uncle's protégé. An award-winning investigative reporter himself. The only person left who could help her.

He looked like he could barely help himself.

Before she could second-guess herself, she stepped up to the table, stopping across from him. "Jason Stone?" She kept her voice low, to prevent anyone from overhearing.

Maybe too low. He didn't move at first, giving no indication he'd heard her. The moment stretched on so long she wondered if she was going to have to repeat herself.

She'd opened her mouth to do so when he slowly lifted his head and leveled bloodshot eyes on her face.

Her breath caught in her throat. Her first thought was that he looked terrible.

Her second was that his photographs hadn't done him justice.

He had at least a couple days' worth of scruff on his face and his hair looked like it hadn't seen a comb in weeks. The eyes that stared back at her were red-rimmed, but it was the misery reflected in them that struck her like a blow, making her stomach twist painfully. And yet, not even his unkempt appearance could hide the fact that this was an exceptionally good-looking man. His face was chiseled, his cheekbones high, those eyes a clear, piercing blue. It was the face of a tragic angel, beautiful even in agony.

"A heartbreaker," Hal had called him more than once. Now that she'd seen him in the flesh, she had no trouble believing it. Cleaned up, and in better days, he must have been irresistible.

All she had to see was the pain in those amazing eyes to know how far he'd fallen from those happier times. Sympathy tugged at her heart. Hal had told her all about that, too. She knew the reason for his pain, knew everything he'd lost. After all these years, he was still grieving.

He lowered his head again. "Whatever it is, lady, I'm not interested."

His voice was surprisingly smooth. The low rumble of it sent a jolt through her system. Finally realizing she was standing there with her mouth open, she clamped her lips together and tried to regain her composure.

Ignoring his comment, she pulled out the chair across from him and slid into the seat. "My name is Audrey Ellison. Hal Talmadge was my uncle."

His hand stilled on the glass in front of him. "Was?"

She winced. "I'm sorry. I thought you might have heard by now. He's dead." The news reports the day after the fire had confirmed that, extinguishing any remaining hope that it might not be true.

Stone didn't say anything for a long moment. Then he slowly began to run the tip of one gloved finger along the rim of his glass. "It was bound to happen someday."

Her hackles rose at the dismissive note in his voice. "He was murdered, Mr. Stone. Someone torched his town house with him in it."

Another long pause, then, "Why are you telling me this?"

"Because I need to know if he talked to you about the book he was working on. The biography of Senator Bridges."

"How is that any of your business?"

"Because whoever killed Hal is after me now, too. The same night he was killed, someone broke into my apartment and attacked me. I barely managed to get away."

"So go to the police."

Audrey all but snorted. "I can't trust the police. You know how powerful Richard Bridges is, all the connections he has. He's going to announce his run for the presidency next week and is the wide favorite to win. Unless, of course, a damaging secret like the one Hal claimed he uncovered comes to light, which is no doubt exactly why his people are taking care of loose ends."

"So release this big secret yourself. Once it's out, Bridges will have other things to worry about than you."

She sighed. "I don't know what it is. Hal talked to me about the project, but only in the most general terms. No details, just that it was about Bridges. You know how secretive he could be, and he was even more determined to keep this one to himself so it didn't leak out. If he did talk to you, then you have to know how excited he was about what he'd uncovered. The way he talked about it, he was convinced it was huge. I know he was almost done with the manuscript, but I'm sure they either took it or it must have been destroyed along with everything else that was in his town house, him included. That's why I'm here. I need to know if he talked to you about it, if you know what it is he found."

Again, he took his time answering, so long that she started to wonder if he would. "He didn't tell me anything more than he told you. General things, no details."

Triumph surged within her. She'd been right. Hal had spoken with him. "Do you have any idea what his discovery could have been? I know you used to cover Bridges."

"No."

"Well, then I guess we'll have to try to figure it out. I'm not sure where to begin—"

"Not interested."

Her gaze sharpened at his words. "I thought Hal was your friend. Don't you care about seeing his killers brought to justice?"

He exhaled sharply. "I gave up on justice a long time ago, lady. It's not my business."

She felt a twinge of regret as she remembered everything she knew about this man's past. No, she supposed she couldn't blame him for feeling that way. "Then how about this? If they came after me, I have to believe they'll come after you. Everybody knows that you were his protégé. Combined with the fact that you used to cover Bridges, they have to suspect he might have discussed the book with you, the same way I did. These people aren't taking any chances. You could be in just as much danger as I am."

"Nobody's come after me yet."

"Probably because they couldn't find you. But if I could, so can they."

"How *did* you find me?"

"Property records. Your building was listed in your uncle's name, and since he died last year and you were his only living relative, I guessed that you probably owned it now."

His nod was terse. "That's one loose end I'll be sure to take care of."

His lack of response stunned her. She gaped at him. "Have you been listening to anything I've been saying?"

"Every word. You just haven't said why I should care."

"Like I said, if they came after me, you have to know they're going to come after you."

He finally lifted those piercing blue eyes to her face once more. "Like I said. Why should I care?"

Her heart plummeted. Looking into his fathomless eyes, she realized the truth.

This wasn't a man who was afraid to die. He'd probably welcome it. He didn't have anything left to live for.

But she did. Hal had been murdered to keep Richard Bridges's secret safe. She had to make sure the truth was told.

Determination pushed down the disappointment at Stone's reaction, giving her a welcome burst of renewed strength. With a tight nod, Audrey pushed herself out of her seat. "I'm sorry I bothered you."

She didn't spare him another glance, putting her back

to him. After three days of searching for Stone, all she'd found was a dead end. She needed a new plan—ASAP. The light pouring from the open doorway now beckoned to her, offering an escape from this miserable place and this man and his pain.

She was on her own. The same way she'd always been.

So be it.

Stone watched the blonde walk away, her head held high and her shoulders squared like a warrior heading into battle. She walked straight to the door. She never looked back.

A familiar sensation hit him in the gut, a roiling emotion he knew all too well. Guilt. Regret. Recrimination. All of the above.

Usually the feeling was accompanied by a rush of memories he couldn't push away. A woman with pale blue eyes and the sweetest smile he'd ever seen.

Two little girls with pigtails and gap-toothed grins.

All dead. Because of him.

This time it was another face that rose in his mind. A woman with shoulder-length blond hair and green eyes, a slightly upturned nose and a stubborn chin. Beautiful, the way Hal had always said she was, albeit more than he'd expected, so much that he'd been inexplicably struck by the sight of her at first. Hers wasn't a smiling visage. The expression burned in his memory was one of disappointment. Almost betrayal.

He reached for his glass and drained it, but still the image didn't fade. He wasn't surprised. It was his first beer of the day, and it had been a long time since alcohol had the power to dull his memories anyway. He mostly came to the bar these days because it was dark and quiet and nobody would bother him, like Mrs. Weston, the neighbor who must have told Audrey Ellison where to find him.

Resentment warred with apprehension inside him. He hated this feeling. He didn't want to get involved, couldn't afford to. That was why he'd given up a career and what was left of his life to pass his days in solitude.

Safe. Away from people and the secrets they kept. Secrets he wanted no knowledge and no part of.

Almost against his will, he looked up. She'd just reached the doorway. She glanced furtively in either direction before slipping outside. Then she was gone.

The feeling gnawing at his insides lingered. He knew better than to get involved, had felt the consequences far too well. Leaving others to their business was the only way he could keep a vague hold on his mental well-being.

None of that mattered. At the moment, all he knew was he wasn't ready to have another life on his conscience, no matter what it cost him in the long run.

Choking back the curse that would draw more attention to him than he wanted, Stone shoved himself up from his seat and started for the exit.

He stopped in the doorway, wincing at the bright afternoon glare. He glanced in both directions, not having seen which way she'd gone.

She'd headed left. He spotted her first, then the car sliding forward down the street a heartbeat later.

His pulse immediately kicked into a higher gear. He

watched in horror, knowing exactly what was about to happen.

She was halfway down the block, preparing to cross the street. Her head was down and the collar of her coat pulled up, no doubt to hide her face. It couldn't give her much in the way of peripheral vision, meaning there was no chance she could see the car inching forward down the street. She glanced both ways before stepping onto the road. Either the car stopped at that moment or she simply didn't see it, because she proceeded forward.

Just as the car did.

He took off at a dead run.

He didn't bother to call out a warning. Shouting out her name would only cause her to stop and look back in surprise. She needed to keep moving. It was the only chance she had.

Then it happened, exactly as he knew it would, when he was still impossibly far away. The car lurched into sudden motion when she was almost to the middle of the street.

At the sound of those squealing tires, she did the instinctive thing, the worst possible thing. She stopped and glanced up, frozen in shock and surprise at the sight of that car barreling toward her. Even if her preservation instinct kicked in, even if she managed to surge into motion, there was little chance she would be able to get out of the way.

His heart exploding, pounding, driving in a way it hadn't in years, he ran as hard and fast as he could, heading straight toward her, even as the car did the same.

And then he was on top of her. He slammed right into her, his arms automatically locking around her, knocking her to the ground. He heard her scream. The noise barely registered among the whirlwind of impressions crowding his senses. They were rolling, over and over, the pavement hard and unforgiving against his back and arms and legs. He felt the rush of wind gusting past as the car blasted by, the roar of its engine drowning out her scream. He felt her in his arms, rigid and yet soft, as soft against his chest as the ground was hard against his back.

Their momentum gradually slowed. They rolled over one last time near the curb. He landed on his side.

His body aching, his chest throbbing, he could barely move. He gradually realized his head was tucked down, his chin resting against the top of hers, her face buried in his chest. Slowly, painfully, he managed to raise his head. He knew he should release her. He couldn't. The tension still gripping his system held him in place, locking his muscles where they were. He could only lie there and peer down at the woman in his arms.

At first she didn't move. Alarm shot through him. He tried to catch his breath, tried to choke out the words to ask if she was all right.

Then she finally shifted. Like someone wakening from a dream, she moved slowly, one limb at a time twitching, testing itself. Finally, she pulled away from his chest and lifted her head. Blinking rapidly, her eyes took a moment to land on his. When they did, they widened even more than they already were. He could read the shock in them, but also see they were clear and focused.

Relief unlike any he'd ever known shuddered through him, rocking his body from head to toe.

He'd made it in time. She was okay. They hadn't gotten her.

Which was what they'd intended. There wasn't a doubt in his mind it had been deliberate. It was exactly what he'd known it was from the instant he'd seen that car. In the back of his mind, he registered what he hadn't heard: the sound of brakes squealing. He'd heard the roar of the engine, the growl constant, uninterrupted. There'd been nothing else with it. He figured if he checked the pavement, he wouldn't find any skidmarks. He wouldn't bother.

It was exactly as she'd said. They'd come after her, whoever "they" were. Bridges's people?

She didn't ask him to let her go. She didn't try to push him off or pull away from him. She simply lay there, her breathing short and rapid, and stared into his eyes.

Sucking in a breath, she finally spoke, her gaze steady and weary and sad.

"Now do you understand how much trouble we're in?"

Chapter Two

"I'm not sure we should be here."

Seated across from Stone in a diner not far from the bar, Audrey eyed her surroundings with unease, especially the large windows on the far walls. Stone had asked for a booth in the back, but Audrey still felt entirely too exposed. Anyone passing by the windows would likely be able to spot them with little difficulty. Every ten seconds or so she felt her gaze drawn back to them. She didn't know what her pursuers looked like, but she somehow expected to find them staring at her through the glass.

"Where exactly should we be?" Stone asked in that laconic way of his.

"Somewhere less public."

"Public's the best place for us now. It's not like they'd make a move on us in here."

"I wouldn't be so sure about that," Audrey muttered, not about to put anything past these people at the moment. The terror of those moments when Stone had crashed into her still hadn't died down, her heart pumping harder and faster than usual, her nerves on edge.

She shifted restlessly in the booth. Her body immediately protested, a thousand little aches and pains making themselves known at various points all over her.

Close. So close. She had no doubt that if it wasn't for Stone, she would be dead right now.

She realized she hadn't thanked him. But looking into his stony expression, she didn't think he would appreciate the sentiment.

"Where else do you want to go?" he asked.

"I don't know." That was the problem. She didn't have any alternatives to offer. They couldn't go back to his place. They couldn't trust that her—their—pursuers hadn't located it, too. It seemed like the only way the pursuers could have caught up with her after she'd managed to avoid them for several days. Even if she'd been spotted on the street, there couldn't have been enough time for them to be contacted and make it to the bar to catch her coming out. More likely they'd followed her from Stone's place to begin with, or Stone's neighbor had told them where to find him just as she had Audrey.

The waitress who'd taken their order finally reappeared, setting two cups of coffee on the table. "Here you go. Do you need anything else?"

"Not right now," Stone said. "Thanks."

Neither of them looked up to watch the waitress walk away. Stone slowly reached for one of the cups and dragged it toward him. "Besides, I need this if I'm going to clear my head enough to think."

She had to concede the point. Chances were, he'd had at least a few beers back at the bar. She was lucky she hadn't found him later in the day. He didn't seem drunk, but he should know his condition better than she would.

Audrey didn't bother reaching for the other cup. She was jumpy enough without the caffeine. Even as she thought it, she couldn't restrain another sweeping glance across the diner, lingering on the windows.

When she returned her attention to Stone, she saw that he hadn't taken a drink from the cup. Instead, he was slowly peeling off the gloves he was wearing.

Audrey knew she should look away, knew exactly what those gloves were concealing, knew it was rude to stare. She glanced away, only to find her attention unerringly drawn back.

The diner's bright fluorescent lights cast an unforgiving glow on his hands, illuminating the thick scars marring his palms. She'd never seen burn marks so severe or so up close. She couldn't even begin to imagine how much it had hurt when they'd been burned.

"Since you don't look surprised, I assume you already know what happened."

Audrey jerked her gaze upward to find him watching her, no expression on his face. So this was a test. She wondered if she'd passed or failed. "Yes," she made herself say as evenly as possible. "I know what happened. Hal told me. I'm so sorry for your loss."

Not a single flicker of emotion passed over his face to acknowledge the loss he'd suffered. But then, there didn't have to be. The man's general appearance was a testament to it. He raised the cup to his mouth, cradling it in those hands. "What exactly did he tell you?" he asked, never taking his eyes from her.

"That your wife and daughters died."

"No," he said simply, a hard edge in his voice. "They didn't die. They were killed. Murdered."

So this is what it's like to be questioned by Jason Stone, she thought as she stared helplessly into the intensity in those eyes. "Yes," she managed to say.

"Did he tell you how?"

Audrey swallowed. "A car bomb."

He arched a brow. "And?"

She hesitated, not sure what he was going for, not sure what to say. "And the bomb was rigged to your car. It was intended for you."

"Because?"

"Because of a story you were working on. Something you were investigating." He'd been looking into a small private defense contractor that was purportedly conducting illegal deals with foreign nationals, something that had proven all too true, something the people involved hadn't wanted revealed.

So they'd set a bomb, one that would have succeeded at its intended purpose, except that at the last minute his wife's car had begun showing signs of engine trouble. So he'd given her the keys to his, kissed his family goodbye and unknowingly sent them to their deaths.

From what Hal had told her, Stone had been inside the house when the car exploded. He'd run outside and thrown himself at the fire, tried to tear one of the doors open to get to his family even though they were likely already long gone by the time he'd gotten out of the house. His hands had been burned by the hot metal as much as by the flames. He'd refused to let go. The neighbors had had to pull him back, fighting the whole way.

It was a horrifying scenario, one she'd had no trouble picturing in vivid detail. A man desperately fighting to save a family that was already gone, burning before his very eyes.

She understood why he'd disappeared of course, though he'd only done so after reporting the story they'd tried to keep him from revealing. It was the only justice his family had received. No one had ever been directly connected to the bombing nor charged with the crime. The only charges brought were those in the original crimes Stone had been investigating. It was reasonable to believe that the people who'd ordered the planting of the bomb had been punished, if only for their lesser crimes. But the person or persons who did the actual bombing remained at large, and would likely remain so.

I gave up on justice a long time ago, lady.

"So you can see why I'm not really interested in playing investigative reporter anymore," he said flatly.

"Yes. But I don't think you have a choice," she said, not without some sympathy. "They're not going to give you one."

From the look that flashed across his face, he couldn't argue with her, and he wasn't any happier about it than she was. He would rather be back in that dingy bar, insulated from the outside world, losing himself in alcohol. She almost couldn't blame him, even as compassion struck for the condition she'd found him in. At least he'd been safe there, from everything but his memories.

And yet, for all he'd lost and all he claimed not to care, he was here now. He'd come after her when he hadn't had to.

It seemed there was still some part of him that was alive, no matter how far beneath the surface it lurked.

"What else do you know about the book?" he asked roughly, a hint of irritation in his tone that he even had to talk about it.

"I know Hal had a title in mind. He wanted to call it *An Honorable Man*."

The corner of his mouth quirked slightly. "I'm assuming the title was intended to be ironic."

"I'm sure. Hal wasn't one for hagiographies, and I doubt he would have been so excited about having found out something wonderful about Bridges."

"There are certainly enough people out there singing the guy's praises."

Stone should know. He'd once been one of those providing the almost universally positive press Bridges had received over the years, a rarity for a politician, to be sure.

"You've met him," she said. "What did you think of him?"

Stone appeared to consider the question. "Honestly, I thought he was a decent guy. I mean, he was a politician to the core, and there's no way to really get a sense of who they are beneath all the smiles and polish. But if I'd had to put money down, I would have said he was a good guy. Just a gut reaction." He shrugged a shoulder. "Guess it just shows, you never can tell."

"No, you can't." Heck, before any of this happened,

she probably would have voted for Richard Bridges herself. The guy had the whole package. In his early fifties, he was handsome, but not so much to turn off men or be dismissed as a pretty boy. He had a quick wit and charm to spare, enough that his appeal crossed party lines, winning opponents to his side while fighting passionately for what he believed in. There'd never been the slightest hint of scandal around him. He'd been married for more than thirty years to the same woman, with whom he had three children. From all appearances, he seemed to be the very thing Hal's title had implied. When Hal had revealed that he'd uncovered something about Bridges, declaring it with a level of glee that told her it had to be something major, she'd actually experienced some doubt that Hal could have found what he thought he had. Richard Bridges had seemed to be that rarest of things—a good man. Unfortunately, like so many others, it seemed he was merely too good to be true.

"Mr. Stone—"

"It's Jason," he said bluntly. "Given the circumstances we might as well be on a first-name basis."

"All right," Audrey agreed. "Jason then. I've been thinking about it. Bridges has spent most of his adult life in the spotlight, with much of it thoroughly covered by the press, especially once it became clear he was going to run for president. If there was anything to be found in his past from the past several decades, someone would have done so by now. He's been gearing up for this presidential run for years, so I have to believe he's been careful, which probably rules out something recent. That leaves his early years as the most likely place where he'd have a skeleton in his closet. I know Hal intended to cover Bridges's full life story in the book, including his childhood and teen years. It makes sense that if he found something, it was in that period."

Stone took a drink from his cup. "That meshes with what Hal told me, how he wanted to learn more about Bridges's early life. I actually don't know much about it beyond the obvious. Who his father is, where he comes from."

Yes, those were pieces of information few people didn't know about. Richard Bridges was actually Richard Bridges, Jr., his father, Dick, having been a long-serving senator from the commonwealth of Virginia before him. The Bridges clan had long been powerful and politically connected in the state. Dick Bridges had had presidential ambitions of his own decades ago, only to find he couldn't expand his popularity far enough beyond his home state. His only son far exceeded him in terms of charisma, and now appeared on the brink of fulfilling the dream his father had failed to realize.

The family homestead was in a small town in Virginia called Barrett's Mill, the same town where Bridges was holding his campaign kickoff event in just three days. The family owned a horse farm there where Richard Bridges had spent his early years before being sent to a fancy prep school, then the University of Virginia, then Harvard Law. Audrey had never heard rumors of anything untoward in those early years. But then, that was the point. Whatever Hal had found, whatever was worth killing him over, was something no one had heard about before.

"What else did Hal tell you?" she asked.

"He wanted to know if I knew anyone who knew Bridges when he was younger who might be willing to talk to him," Stone said. "I told him to contact Gabe Franklin."

Audrey frowned. "Who's that?"

"He's a lawyer, a big name when it comes to constitutional law. He lives here in D.C. and teaches at Georgetown. Most important, he went to prep school with Bridges. I don't know if Franklin gave him anything. We should talk to him and find out. If he did give Hal something, it might be something we should know."

"Sounds good." It sounded more than good. It was exactly what she'd hoped for, that Stone could provide the knowledge and contacts she lacked to get to the bottom of this.

"Of course, there's the matter of how Bridges and his people found out that Hal had found anything, given how secretive he was being."

"Maybe there was a leak in his agent's or publisher's office."

"Maybe," he said, leaving the possibility up in the air. Because there was no way to know for sure. Audrey shook her head with a sigh. So many questions, and after three days she wasn't any closer to answers.

The thought made her uneasy, and she couldn't help but do another check of the windows.

And then she saw him, a man standing on the other side of the glass, staring right at her.

He was a big man, forty-something, with a buzz cut and blunt features. She must have glanced in his direction at just the right moment. Their eyes met across the distance. He almost immediately looked away, but not before she saw the hard edge in his stare and knew without the slightest doubt who he was.

It was just as she'd thought. They'd been found.

With some effort, she forced her throat to move, to make sounds. "Jason—"

"I saw him," he said before she could say anything. "Let's go."

"What—" She looked at him in surprise to find that he was already sliding out of the booth, tossing a few bills on the table to cover the coffees.

She didn't even have a chance to ask where he expected them to go before Stone was on his feet and standing beside the booth with his hand, encased in its glove again, extended. He kept his eyes on the window. She followed his gaze. The window was empty, the man she'd seen there now nowhere in sight. But she had no doubt he was out there, just waiting for them to emerge.

"Come on," Stone said with a trace of impatience.

The urgency in the order propelled her into motion. She grabbed her bag and moved to the end of the booth. As soon as she was standing, he took her arm and pulled her forward. He didn't head to the front door as she expected, walking instead to the back of the diner.

A hallway in the rear of the building led to some restrooms and what appeared to be an emergency exit. Bright red letters affixed to the door indicated that an alarm would go off if it was opened.

She started to ask if it was a good idea to use the door,

but before she could get a word out, he turned abruptly, plowing through a swinging door to their left, pulling her with him.

Then they were in the kitchen. "Are we allowed back here?" she asked without thinking.

"Who cares?" he said shortly, hurrying through the room toward a door in the back, this one with no warning on it.

Out of the corner of her eye, she saw a cook behind a counter glance up as they passed, his mouth falling open slightly. Judging from his expression, they definitely weren't allowed back here. Before he could say anything, they'd already zipped past him.

Stone finally slowed as they approached the door. He eased it open with one hand, carefully scanning whatever lay on the other side of the gap he created. In the next moment, he released her arm, pushing his upper body through the opening and glancing behind the door as well.

Seemingly reassured, he stepped back into the room and retook her arm. "Come on."

Shoving the door open entirely, he pulled her through it, into an alley. He led her to the left, down the enclosed space ripe with the smell of garbage and cluttered with debris. She almost asked if he'd considered whether the man would expect them to exit through the back or if he might have a partner lying in wait. One glance at the resolute expression on his face, his eyes narrowed, his features tense, and she knew there was little he hadn't considered.

Stone kept checking behind them, no doubt keeping

an eye out, should their pursuers suddenly appear. She couldn't help but do the same. The alley opened onto another. To her surprise, Stone suddenly slowed, then stopped completely in front of a door. She watched as he inserted a key he already had in hand into the lock, then pushed the door open. It was a garage, she realized, seconds before he pulled her through the opening.

A single vehicle—a sedan whose features she could barely make out—was parked inside the cramped space. Stone closed and locked the door behind them before moving to the driver's side of the car. "Get in," he said.

Audrey obeyed, immediately moving to the passenger side. "Whose car is this?"

"Mine," he said tersely.

She climbed in, her eyes automatically returning to his face as he started the engine. "You park this far from your apartment?"

"It's not that far."

No, she realized, it probably wasn't. The diner was likely midway between his building and the bar. The garage had to be at least several blocks from his apartment, but it wasn't an extreme distance.

As for why he'd chosen to park in a garage away from the building, she didn't have to ask. Considering what had happened with his family, it made sense. As unlikely as it was that the same thing would happen again, he wasn't going to park in the open, and he wouldn't want anyone to easily locate his vehicle.

Audrey watched him reach up and push the button on

a garage door opener clipped to the visor. "You should stay down, just in case," he said.

She ducked down in her seat and listened to the sound of the garage door raising. She sensed more than saw the tension in Stone's body, and knew he was completely on guard.

He slowly pulled out of the garage, turning right onto the street. Within moments, the vehicle picked up speed. Holding her breath, she waited for some sign he'd spotted the man from the diner, or worse, that they'd been spotted themselves.

When she felt Stone relax almost imperceptibly, she knew it was safe. She was already sitting up when he said, "We're clear."

"Now what?" she asked softly.

"Now we go see Franklin."

Audrey didn't bother to ask what they'd do about her car. Obviously, it had to be left where it was. If she had been followed to the bar, her pursuers would clearly know where she'd parked. After failing to hit her, they could have gone back and placed a tracking device on the vehicle, intending to follow wherever she went.

Now she really had nothing, she thought bleakly. All she had left was what she had on her.

She did her best to push aside the sadness that threatened to well up again, focusing instead on how deliberate Jason's plan had been.

"That was some quick thinking. If I didn't know better, I'd think you'd been prepared for just this eventuality."

"I always prepare for anything," he said grimly.

Ever since he'd lost his family, she realized. He'd been blindsided, had failed to protect those he loved most. He wasn't going to be caught off guard again.

He'd thought this might happen. It was the real reason he'd chosen the diner. He'd planned for this, giving her no indication that was the case. She couldn't help but wonder what else he wasn't sharing with her and eye him more closely as a result.

Brilliant, Hal had called him. *Razor sharp.* She'd just had no idea how much so.

And for the first time it occurred to her that, beyond the information he could provide her with, this might be a good man to have on her side.

Chapter Three

They'd gotten away.

Albert Shaw scanned the street one last time, even though he knew it wouldn't make a difference. He didn't know how Stone and the Ellison woman had done it, but they clearly had.

They were gone.

A faint trace of anger flickered deep in his gut, the feeling too muted to make much of an impact. He wasn't happy about this development, but he'd learned long ago to maintain absolute control over his emotions. Feelings could only interfere with getting the job done.

This particular job was to eliminate Stone and the Ellison woman. This setback aside, he intended to complete it.

From his vantage point in the front of the restaurant, he'd caught sight of them heading to the back, but by the time he'd made it to the alley behind the diner there'd been no sign of them. They'd either doubled back and left through the front after all, or they'd somehow made it down the alley before he could follow. Their escape route didn't matter. All that did was finding them again—and fast.

Shaw turned quickly and headed back to his vehicle. He could cover more ground faster in his car. It would give him an advantage if they were on foot.

His cell phone vibrated. He checked the screen just long enough to ID the caller—Bridges—then ignored the device. He was going to hold off on talking to the man as long as possible, preferably until he had something to report. Bridges wasn't going to be happy Stone and Ellison were still out there any more than Shaw was.

He frowned, the anger nearly managing to burst through to the surface. The fact that they were still out there made him look sloppy, inept, and he took too much pride in his work to be happy about that. He always planned everything out completely, methodically. But this job had gone bad from the start. His initial assignment had simply been to obtain a copy of Talmadge's book before he turned it in, so Bridges could determine if any action needed to be taken before its contents spread beyond Talmadge and the few he may have discussed it with. Eliminating Talmadge was a last resort, something that needed to be avoided if at all possible, because it was sure to look suspicious.

Shaw had hired an associate to hack into Talmadge's computer, but it had turned out Talmadge had been writing his book on a laptop that wasn't connected to the internet—to keep himself from being distracted, or because he thought someone might try to hack it? Either way, Shaw had been forced to access the laptop himself. But when Talmadge had finally left his home and given Shaw the opportunity to break in, he'd returned earlier than expected. There'd been no way to get out of the house before Talmadge noticed, and when the man had found him, drastic measures had been required. Rather than simply leaving with the copy of the book he'd downloaded onto a flash drive, Shaw had had to terminate the man, using the fire to both cover the murder and destroy Talmadge's work.

Shaw didn't regret the action. It had been unavoidable. What he did regret was the timing. If he'd had time to prepare, he would have tracked down Stone before acting, and Talmadge, Ellison and Stone all would have died on the same night, everything tied up neatly. Shaw had been monitoring the man's phone and email communications and knew that Talmadge's editor and agent didn't know what was in the book. Talmadge didn't have much of a social life, and based on his phone records, in the past year he'd only had lengthy conversations with two people: Ellison and Stone. If he'd told anyone what was in the book, it would have been them. They were the only possible loose ends.

Finally reaching his vehicle, Shaw climbed in, the memory of how close he'd been to taking out Ellison making him grimace. It would have been easier if he'd been able to open fire and simply take out the Ellison woman on the street. In a neighborhood like this, a drive-by wouldn't raise an eyebrow. But it would be better if her death looked like an accident. Too many people knew what Hal Talmadge had been working on—the subject if not the specifics. It was going to look suspicious enough having Talmadge and those closest to him die within days of each other. It would be worse if any of those deaths appeared to be direct hits. People would definitely take a closer look at the good senator then, maybe start wondering whether Talmadge had been on to something after all, possibly start trying to re-create his work. That was exactly what couldn't be allowed to happen.

No, their deaths—both Stone's and Ellison's—would appear as accidental as Hal Talmadge's when they happened. And they *would* happen.

They may have escaped him for the moment, but that didn't change the fact that they were living on borrowed time.

Shaw shoved his key in the ignition, but rather than start the engine, he sat there thinking quickly. Driving the streets randomly trying to spot them would most likely be a waste of time. He needed a better plan. He'd found Ellison this time by figuring she'd look for Stone. His best bet was to figure out where they'd go next.

If Audrey Ellison had a copy of the book or knew what was in it, she would have gone to the press instead of looking for Stone. The fact that she hadn't told him all he needed to know. As for Stone, Shaw had to operate under the assumption that he didn't know what was in it, either. If he did, then the situation was likely too late to contain anyway.

But if Stone didn't know, then he and Ellison would most likely try to figure out what it was Talmadge had dug up. To do that, they would have to re-create Talmadge's investigation.

Which meant Shaw had an advantage.

Smiling slowly, he pulled out the flash drive containing Talmadge's book.

A little homework and he'd know where they were going before they did.

GABE FRANKLIN LIVED in a three-story town house in Cleveland Park. Jason parked down the block in a space shadowed by trees. Night had fallen during the drive there, and between the trees and the lack of direct light from any nearby streetlamps, the car was covered in darkness as much as possible. Audrey doubted anyone was looking for the car; Jason hadn't said whose name it was registered under, but she knew it wasn't his. Still, she suspected he was right and it was better to keep the vehicle as inconspicuous as they could.

They quickly made their way to Franklin's building and climbed the steps to the front door. Jason rang the bell. Audrey could hear the sound of the chimes echoing deep into the recesses of the house. "How much do you plan to tell him?" she asked.

"Only as much as I have to."

She didn't have time to ask any further questions when the door suddenly swung open. The man who stood there appeared to be in his mid-fifties, with thick gray hair that gave him a distinguished look and piercing clear blue eyes. The way he was dressed, in a button-down shirt open at the neck with the sleeves rolled up and no shoes, made him look very much at home. Audrey had to assume this was Gabe Franklin.

He didn't even look at her, those eyes automatically going to the man beside her and widening slightly in surprise. "Stone?"

Jason nodded tersely. "It's been a while, Franklin."

Eyebrows lifting, Franklin scanned Stone from head to toe. "You look like hell."

"I see you're still not pulling any punches."

"I've never really seen the point."

"Glad to hear it. We need to talk to you."

"About what?"

"Can we come in?"

Franklin's eyes narrowed as though he'd like an answer first. Something in the seriousness of Stone's tone must have gotten through, because after a moment he nodded and stepped aside.

As soon as they were inside the entryway, he closed the door and turned to face them. "Now what is this about?"

Stone sent a glance toward the interior of the house. "Are you alone?"

"No, you're here," Franklin said archly. "But there's no one else if that's what you mean."

"We're here about Hal Talmadge."

"He's dead."

A wry grin curved one side of Stone's mouth. "Believe us, we definitely know. This is Hal's niece, Audrey Ellison."

Franklin's gaze finally flickered over to her. "I'm sorry for your loss," he said by rote, with no inflection whatsoever.

"Thank you," Audrey said, matching his flatness.

"I'm sure you know Talmadge was working on a biography of Richard Bridges," Stone said.

"Sure."

"Did he get in touch with you to interview you for the book?"

"You should know. You sent him to me."

"Did you talk to him?"

"Briefly," Franklin said slowly, a clear note of caution in his tone.

"Most of Hal's work was destroyed in the fire that killed him. Audrey and I both know how much the book meant to him. Audrey would like to make sure it's completed. She came to me, and I agreed to help her with the project."

Franklin raised a brow. "And this is something you needed to make sure no one overheard us talking about?"

"We would prefer that word didn't get out until we know if we can complete the project. Besides, Hal always believed in discretion. It seems in his spirit to operate under the same philosophy. In any case, we're trying to re-create his research, and since we thought he spoke with you early in the process, this seemed like a good place to start."

For a long moment, Franklin simply stared at Jason through narrowed eyes. Audrey couldn't tell whether or not he believed Jason's story. Finally, he simply turned and moved into a room to the right of the entryway. "You might as well have a seat."

They followed him into what appeared to be a living room area. The walls were covered with framed photographs of Franklin with an array of famous and prominent faces. Audrey reflexively glanced toward the windows on the front wall, relaxing slightly when she saw the curtains were closed.

Motioning toward the seating area, Franklin moved toward a bar on the opposite wall. "Can I get you anything?"

They both declined, Audrey taking a seat on the couch, Stone in the chair closest to her. Audrey pulled a pen and notepad out of her bag. She didn't want to miss anything Franklin told them, and she figured the man would probably expect her to take notes anyway.

"What did you and Hal talk about?" Stone asked.

"He wanted to know what Bridges was like in prep school," Franklin answered over his shoulder. "Everything I remembered about those days."

"And what did you tell him?"

Franklin finally returned, drink in hand, and carefully lowered himself into the chair opposite Stone. "Nothing that wasn't already common knowledge or that he couldn't have learned elsewhere. I had the feeling he knew most of it. In those days, Bridges was a nice enough guy, but nothing special, really. Almost all of us had fathers pushing us to succeed, but Bridges didn't really care about that. He wasn't ambitious, didn't do anything to distinguish himself as far as I can remember. Out of all the young men in our class, Bridges was just about the last I would have predicted getting as far as he did. He just didn't seem to have the drive or the desire. I was a little surprised when he got into Yale—though I'm sure Dick Bridges played a large part in that—but wasn't surprised at all when he didn't arrive on campus that fall with the rest of our class who was going there."

"He was expected to go to Yale?" Audrey asked.

"Originally, yes. The next thing I heard was that he'd deferred and decided to travel in Europe for a year, and when he came back the following year he went to the University of Virginia instead. Clearly the year away did him a lot of good. From all reports he came back more focused, more driven, displaying many of the qualities that have led him to where he is today."

Now that he mentioned it, Audrey remembered

hearing the same thing about Richard Bridges's youth. He'd made it part of his personal story, how he'd been rather aimless in his younger days, until the year he'd spent abroad in Europe before he started college. Seeing the world had opened his eyes to his place in it, and started his interest in public service and his desire to make a difference.

It was a nice story, a young man finding himself and turning his life around. Audrey hadn't thought about it much. She hadn't had a reason to. Now, though, she couldn't help but turn it over in her mind and wonder if there wasn't more to it.

Audrey spoke up. "Do you remember Bridges having any particular interest in traveling abroad when you knew him?"

Rather than answer, Franklin smiled faintly and took a sip from his drink.

"What is it?" Stone asked.

"Talmadge asked me the same thing," Franklin said. He glanced at Audrey. "I guess you really are his niece. But the answer is no. The only place I ever remember him talking about was that town in Virginia where he grew up. He liked it there, liked the horses on their farm. Probably no surprise considering how he's still well-known for loving horses. I believe he went back there every summer. I don't recall ever hearing of him traveling anywhere else."

Audrey wasn't surprised to hear how much Bridges loved his hometown, since he'd chosen to launch his presidential campaign there in a few days.

"Do you know if he went back there the summer after

you both graduated from prep school, before he left for Europe?" Jason asked.

"As far as I know. I remember how surprised everyone was when we heard that he'd decided to travel the continent, so I doubt that he mentioned it or that anyone had the slightest idea. And I can't imagine where he could have gone before that, besides the town in Virginia."

So he'd gone to the hometown that he loved, and at the end of the summer, rather than stay there or go to college as he'd planned, he left for Europe. And once he came back, he'd decided to attend a different college altogether. Audrey had to wonder how that had all come about and why.

"Is there anything else you remember telling Hal that you haven't mentioned?" Jason asked.

Franklin hesitated, a trace of wariness crossing his features. "There was one story, but I told it to him with the understanding that he wouldn't reveal me as his source."

Jason nodded. "We can promise you the same."

Franklin looked at him for a long moment, as though weighing whether to believe him, then finally sighed and opened his mouth again. Audrey had to resist the urge to lean forward in excitement.

"It was a minor incident, really, and frankly it says more about Dick Bridges than Rich. In any case, the most vivid memory I have of both Bridgeses is from one of those family weekends when the parents came to the school to visit. Most of the students had accomplishments to show off. You know, prizes they'd won, achievements they made. Rich didn't. As I said, he never made much of an impression in school. At one point during the weekend, I came across the two of them in an out-of-the-way spot where Dick had evidently pulled Rich aside. Dick was berating him, basically screaming at him about how he wasn't living up to his name and how he had a responsibility to both himself and his father." Franklin shrugged. "It was the sort of thing most of us had had ingrained in us from an early age. Except that Rich started yelling back, about how he didn't care about his name, how he wasn't Dick and never would be, how he didn't even want to be there—that sort of thing. He only stopped when Dick suddenly slapped him across the face. Dick became very quiet, and he said in this incredibly cold tone that he didn't care. Rich was his son, and Dick didn't care what he wanted. He was going to do whatever Dick told him to."

Franklin shook his head with a shrug. "I didn't stick around to hear any more. I never was one for uncomfortable scenes, and I'd heard more than enough. I suppose it's not much of a story anyway. Dick Bridges was the kind of father who was pushing his son hard. That's no secret. And it all worked out. All that pushing got Rich where he is today. In all likelihood, Dick's son is going to be our next president."

Yes, Audrey thought, it was certainly no secret how ambitious Dick Bridges was, nor how much his son's success meant to him. Rich Bridges was fulfilling his father's dream after Dick had never achieved his own presidential ambitions. The main reason Dick Bridges's career had never gone further was that he simply wasn't very likable. He didn't have his son's natural charisma. He came across as cold, arrogant. Even when he was being friendly, it seemed slightly forced, like he was pretending. He just didn't seem like a very nice man. Franklin's story was entirely believable. She could easily imagine Dick as a man who'd berate and slap his son because he wasn't doing what he wanted him to.

Yet, now he was about to get exactly what he wanted. He'd managed to get his son to fall in line, and Rich Bridges was on the verge of becoming president. And it seemed Rich had inherited his father's unwillingness to let anything stop him from getting what he wanted, she realized with a shudder.

And now she and Stone were the only things left standing in his way.

"WHAT DO YOU THINK?" Audrey asked as they left Franklin's town house and headed back to the car.

"I'm thinking there's more to this Europe story," Jason said. "I never considered how unusual it was before. Actually, I never really thought about that element of his history at all."

"I know it's common for students from other countries to take a year off to travel and do other things before college, but it's still pretty rare in the U.S. It certainly would have been thirty-five years ago."

"Not to mention Dick Bridges doesn't sound like the kind of father who would be willing to let his son take a year off instead of going to college."

"So you have to wonder why he did," Audrey concluded. "There may be more to the story."

"And if Hal started thinking about why Bridges went to Europe, what would he have done?"

Audrey didn't even have to think about it. "He would

have gone to Barrett's Mill to see if he could find out whether something happened that summer that would have led to Bridges going away."

Jason nodded. "Which is exactly what we have to do."

She glanced at him. "But when? We can't go now. With Bridges announcing his presidential run in just a few days, the place is going to be overrun with reporters and Bridges's staff."

"We can't exactly wait. There's someone out there trying to track us down, with every intention of killing us. We need to figure out what Hal had ASAP. It's the only chance of putting an end to this before Bridges's man gets to us."

"But it's a small town. It won't be easy keeping a low profile and not having anyone recognize us."

They'd reached the car. He stopped and looked at her, his eyebrows lifting slightly, the corners of his mouth quirking in the beginnings of a smile. "Then I guess we'll need some disguises."

The words barely registered, the sight of that near-smile catching her completely off guard and overshadowing everything else. She couldn't think, couldn't begin to process any new information. She could only stare helplessly into his face as the breath lodged in her throat, her heart doing a strange lurch in her chest, then quickly picking up speed.

It certainly wasn't much of a smile, just a slight curving of his mouth, combined with a wry sparkle in his eyes, yet somehow that only added to its impact, giving it a lazy quality that only made it sexier. It transformed him, freeing his features from the pain and tension that had weighed on him from the moment she'd met him. With them, he'd still been incredibly good-looking; without them, he was absolutely devastating. For the first time, she caught a glimpse of the dashing Jason Stone she'd heard so much about, and he was every bit as promised.

Wow.

The smile gradually faded, the amused gleam in his eyes replaced by something else, something that sent a fresh rush of emotion shooting through her. His gaze slowly stroked over her face. She couldn't read his expression, couldn't tell what he was thinking as she peered up at him. She could barely think herself as she stood there under his scrutiny, her heart pounding in her chest, her mouth bone-dry as his eyes pored over her with painstaking thoroughness. It was as though he was searching for something, though she couldn't imagine what.

He finally lowered his gaze, severing the connection between them so quickly she nearly rocked back on her heels from the shock of it. "We should get a move on," he said roughly. "If we're going to do this, we have a lot to take care of tonight."

Audrey cleared her throat. "Right," she said, hoping her voice didn't sound nearly as strained to his ears as it did to her own. "Let's go."

Without another glance at her, Stone headed toward the driver's side of the vehicle. Audrey took a deep breath before moving, trying to understand what had just happened, the reaction she'd just had, the strength of it. It was inexplicable. It made no sense given the circumstances.

Yet it had been there all the same. Attraction. Awareness. Something much fiercer than anything she'd felt in a long time, the feeling as devastating as the man who'd so briefly stood before her. The memory of it was enough to bring the feeling back to her and send her adrenaline spiking.

She drew in another breath and did her best to shake off the feeling. They didn't have time for this. She was coasting on fumes, surviving on too much coffee and too little sleep. Obviously, she wasn't thinking clearly. That was all it was. She just needed to get some rest.

She chose to ignore the fact that she'd never felt more awake in the past three days than she did right now. Her heart was thudding, her skin was practically buzzing. Her body certainly wanted something all right—but sleep wasn't it.

Not by a long shot.

Chapter Four

Seated at her dressing table, Julia Bridges stared into the mirror and watched her husband pack his suitcase on the bed behind her. She let a smile play against her lips, hoping the expression sufficiently hid her unease.

"We're not leaving for a few days," she said with a lightness that sounded false to her ears. "I don't think I've ever seen you pack for a trip so early."

"It's going to be a busy few days," Rich said absently, without looking at her. "I'd rather take care of it now, while I have some time, than to have to do it at the last minute."

"I could have done it for you. I've done it before," she pointed out.

"That's not necessary. I can do it myself."

There was no harshness in the words. There was nothing at all as he continued placing clothes in the bag.

Despite her words, she wasn't really surprised by his actions. He did always like to be prepared, and they were heading into one of the biggest days of his life.

This time though, she wouldn't mind if he wasn't quite so efficient. His actions only reminded her of what was coming, where they were going, and she would never be completely prepared for that.

They were going to Barrett's Mill, that godawful little town she would love to never set foot in again. If there was any way she could avoid it, she would.

But then, she'd learned long ago that sometimes a person had to do exactly what was necessary, no matter how distasteful, to get what they wanted.

Oh, yes, she thought as she met her clear gaze in the mirror. She was an expert when it came to that.

So she would go back there with him. She would stand behind him as he announced his intention to run for the presidency. She would smile and shake hands and pose for a million pictures. Then she would get out of that town the first possible moment.

If Rich felt the slightest discomfort himself about going back there, he didn't show it. But then, he had no reason to. He'd been in on the decision to begin the campaign there from the beginning.

Not to mention he wasn't showing her much of anything lately. He'd withdrawn into himself over the past few days, the closer they came to the big event and the announcement everyone was expecting and waiting for. In public, he was the same genial, charismatic figure he always was, but when they were alone, he was distracted, closed off. He seldom confided in her anymore, barely spoke at all. She couldn't tell what he was thinking.

It was an uncomfortable feeling that put her on edge. She knew their marriage hadn't gotten off to the best start—he hadn't wanted to marry her; she'd simply left him no choice. But in the years since, the bond between them had grown and strengthened. She was the one person who knew him better than any other, who kept all his secrets just as she'd promised when she married him. He knew he could trust her more than anyone else.

Or so she'd thought. But now he seemed to be pulling away, retreating into himself at the worst possible time. This was everything they'd worked toward for so long, the end result of everything they'd done. They were so close. She wished he would look at her, smile at her, give her some indication everything would be all right.

He did none of those things. He finished packing the bag, zipped it up and placed it on the floor, then moved into the closet to retrieve another. Not once did he glance in her direction, nor did he say a word as he turned and walked away from her.

Staring at his retreating back, Julia fought another ripple of unease.

She always thought she knew him better than anyone, but at times like these she wondered if she really knew him at all.

STONE HESITATED before opening the motel room door, his fingers tightening on the paper bag clenched in his right hand. He sent a glance behind him to make sure no one was paying him any particular attention, but didn't see anyone. The lot was nearly empty, with only a couple cars parked in front of the building. He didn't think he'd been followed back to the motel, but he couldn't be too cautious.

He still paused before entering the room, though he knew full well his reluctance had nothing to do with the potential presence of any watchers.

After leaving D.C., they'd headed into Virginia,

stopping to buy some clothes and materials to disguise their appearances, then checking in to a motel on the way to Barrett's Mill. Stone had left Audrey to clean up and change while he went out to get some food. He could have picked up the food when they'd made the rest of their purchases, but he needed some time away from her. He had to figure out how to broach the topic that had been weighing on his mind since they'd left D.C.

A half hour later, he was no closer to an answer.

She wasn't going to like what he had to say.

That wasn't going to keep him from saying it.

With a sigh, he unlocked the door and pushed it open. "I'm back," he said immediately, so she wouldn't be concerned. At first there was no answer. The room was small, barely big enough to fit the two single beds, and she was nowhere in sight. His eyes automatically went to the open bathroom door, a light shining inside it. "Audrey?"

"In here," her voice, slightly muffled, came from the bathroom.

The sound was muted, barely audible, and a whisper of concern slid through him. Why did she sound like that? Was something wrong?

Dropping the bag on the dresser next to the TV, he quickly and quietly made his way across the room and rounded the end of the far bed to reach the bathroom door. Nerves on alert, he slowly leaned over and peered inside.

And came to a dead stop.

She was fine. She was more than fine. She stood in front of the bathroom mirror, her eyes pinned on her reflection as she slowly worked her fingers through her hair. The smell he'd barely registered as he'd approached the bathroom finally sank in. It was hair dye. She was coloring her hair with the dye they'd bought on the way there, changing it from blond to dark brown. She'd cut her hair so it barely reached the nape of her neck, but it was still thick, and from the furrowing of her brow and the way she was gently biting her lip, she wasn't having the easiest time of it. She was concentrating carefully on what she was doing. That was the reason for her muffled answer, nothing more.

As soon as he realized she was all right, he should have backed away from the door and left her alone. He knew it. But knowing it didn't get his legs to move or his eyes to look away.

She was wearing only a thin T-shirt and a pair of shorts that barely reached midthigh. The shirt clung to her curves, clearly outlining every one. Even as he registered that fact, she shifted her weight and the bottom of the shorts slid higher, drawing his attention and revealing a few more centimeters of thigh. His gaze frozen, he looked a hell of a lot longer than he had any business doing before he managed to drag his eyes back to her face.

He still couldn't move, tension spreading through him and holding him in place. It seemed like he could barely swallow, his throat too damn tight. As he watched her struggle with the dye, he had a feeling she hadn't done this before. With hair the color of hers—that rich natural blond so many others dyed *their* hair to achieve— she'd probably never felt the need. Some of the dye had already dripped onto the shoulders of her T-shirt. He guessed that must be why she was wearing so little when he knew he'd bought her more clothes than what she had on. She likely hadn't wanted to risk ruining too much of her limited wardrobe.

The urge rose within him to step forward and offer to help her. It was the decent thing to do. But there was nothing decent about the feeling that spiked through him at the mere thought of moving his hands through her hair, of listening to the soft hitch of her breath as he worked the strands through his fingers, of being that close to her...

He recognized the feeling all too well. It was the same feeling he'd had on the street outside Franklin's house when he'd suddenly found himself peering into her eyes. The heat spreading through his system. The tightness in his chest.

Yeah, he recognized the feeling. He just didn't know why the hell it was happening now.

Okay, she was an attractive woman. A lot more than just attractive, if he wanted to be honest about it—which he damn well didn't. He understood that much. But it had been a long time since he'd felt anything for any woman, let alone something this strong. Well over two years now. Ever since Lisa died.

No. Ever since Lisa was murdered, and Megan and Morgan with her.

The reminder slammed into him, bringing back the pain, the guilt. It should have been enough to kill his reaction to this woman, but it wasn't. Not entirely.

He hadn't felt much of anything since that day. Never really thought he would again. Hadn't wanted to, either.

And yet here it was, because of a woman he'd just met. He couldn't explain it. He damn well didn't like it.

All the more reason to say what he needed to.

"Everything okay?" she asked suddenly, without taking her eyes off the mirror. "Did you find some food?"

He blinked, startled, and wondered how long he'd been standing there before she'd decided to say something. He somehow managed to make his throat move. "Yeah."

"Spot any trouble?"

"No."

"Then why do you sound so uneasy?"

He grimaced. Cues didn't come much better than that. "Look, I've been thinking…"

"About what?" she prompted after a moment when he didn't continue.

"About what you said earlier about how risky it is to be going to Barrett's Mill."

"You don't want to go anymore?"

"No, I'm not sure *you* should go. It might be too dangerous. It would be safer if we found a place for you to hole up for a while until I get to the bottom of this."

She arched a brow. "So I get to sit around twiddling my thumbs and slowly going out of my mind, waiting for someone to either kill me or for you to take care of everything for me? No thanks."

"I can handle this myself."

"I'm sure you can, but the two of us working on this means we're likely to get to the bottom of it twice as fast." She shot him a look in the mirror. "I'm not completely without experience, you know. I was a journalism major in college and worked for three years at a daily paper."

Yes, he did know that. He knew a lot more about her than he suspected she had any idea of. She was an only child. After her parents were killed in a small plane crash when she was eleven, she was given over to the custody of her sole remaining relative, Hal, her maternal uncle. Hal hadn't known what to do with an eleven-year-old girl, not to mention that he'd always been far too busy with his career to have time for anyone else, which was one reason he never married. So he sent her to an exclusive boarding school where she'd spent the next seven years, before graduating and advancing to college. She seldom spent holidays with Hal, and most summers he'd managed to find some camp or program to send her to, rather than have her come home to him. It was partly why Jason was a little surprised at how determined she was to participate in the investigation. He knew she and Hal hadn't been close. But then, this wasn't just about Hal. Her life was at risk because of this, too.

Yes, she'd been a reporter, but she'd given it up to become a family photographer. She had her own small studio in Baltimore. "That was years ago," he said. "You quit."

She met his eyes in the mirror. "So did you," she pointed out gently. "There are other reasons for quitting a job besides not being good at it. I didn't quit because I couldn't hack it, if that's what you're worried about. I was good at my job. My bosses liked me, and I was working my way up pretty quickly."

"So why quit?"

She glanced away, and he watched her swallow before answering. "Because I realized it wasn't what I wanted to do. It wasn't my passion. I was doing it for the wrong reasons."

The reporter in him almost asked what those reasons were, before he recognized they were none of his business.

"That's not going to be an issue here," Audrey continued. "Believe me, I have plenty of passion when it comes to this investigation. It's my life that's on the line here, it was my uncle who was murdered. I'm not quitting until the truth is revealed and Bridges has paid for what he's done."

He wouldn't have expected her to say anything else. That didn't mean he was happy about it, or intended to give up so easily.

Before he could try a different approach, she spoke first. "You know," she began, her tone instantly making him wary. "If you're worried about the danger, maybe you should hole up somewhere while *I* go to Barrett's Mill by myself. After all, Bridges and his people aren't going to be the only ones in town. Barrett's Mill is going to be full of members of the media, some of whom will be your former colleagues. Don't you think some of them will recognize you?"

"That's why I bought some hair dye for myself, too," he pointed out.

"Changing your hair from brown to black isn't much of a disguise."

"I also bought those sunglasses. I'll keep them on whenever we're in public. I've lost some weight over the past few years, so my face is leaner than it used to be. Put it all together, and that should enough to keep me from being recognized."

Her eyes darted toward him in the mirror, flickering nervously over his face before moving away again. "I don't know. I think you may be underestimating how… noticeable you are."

From the hesitancy in both her words and her gaze, Stone had no trouble understanding what she meant. Women had reacted like that to him before. He'd never been one for false modesty, and he knew he was what most people would consider a handsome man. Or at least he had been. At one time it had mattered to him, and he'd taken great care with his appearance, as arrogant about that as he'd been about everything else. But it had been a long time since he'd given the slightest thought to his appearance, barely able to look at himself in the mirror. Given the way he felt, he wouldn't have thought he still qualified as good-looking.

But clearly she thought he did. He watched her cheeks redden slightly in the mirror, and a jolt shot through him. He knew immediately that whatever it was he'd felt at Franklin's house, she'd felt it, too. And she felt it now, the same way he did, the awareness hanging in the air between them.

He choked back a curse, even as his pulse kicked into a higher gear. Even more reason why they would be better off splitting up.

"We're not talking about me," he said. "We're talking about you. I still think you would be safer—"

She raised her chin. "If we're talking about danger, we *should* be talking about you. I'm not going to be completely safe no matter where I am, so I might as well go. But you're much more recognizable than I am, so the danger is greater for you. So if you're that worried about danger, you can stay behind. I would understand. But I'm going."

Her jaw tight, she focused her attention on the mirror, her tense body language daring him to argue with her.

Oh, hell. She had him and she knew it. A reluctant grin nearly pulled at the corner of his mouth before he killed the impulse. He'd known she was smart and tough. Hal had told him that much. They may not have spent much time together, but it seemed Hal had known exactly who she was.

There was obviously no way he was letting her go on to Barrett's Mill by herself. There was no question it was going to be risky, but it was a risk that needed to be taken. By both of them, it seemed.

Damn it.

"Fine," he said, barely managing to keep the frustration from his tone, "we'll both go."

She displayed none of the smugness he might have expected at getting her way. Instead, after a long moment, her eyes slowly slid to his. And held.

His tension returned in a burst. He could tell from her expression she felt it, too, and was equally uneasy about it. It suddenly occurred to him that maybe she hadn't been trying to convince him to let her come, as he'd assumed. Maybe she really had been trying to ditch him the same way he'd been trying to ditch her. Evidently, neither of them wanted to stay too close to the other. The idea gave him no pleasure. It just meant they were both going to have to deal with whatever this inexplicable thing was between them.

Her gaze finally slid away again. "Good," she said. "I'm almost done in here and the room will be all yours."

"Great." With some effort, this time he did manage to make himself turn away. He moved back to the door of the room and fastened the chain, checking that the lock was bolted. Going to the window, he pushed the curtain aside slightly with the tip of one finger, just enough that he could get a decent view of the scene outside. The parking lot remained clear. No cars appeared to have arrived since he'd come in, and no one was in sight. It looked like they were still safe for the moment.

So why did he feel anything but?

Probably because he could still sense her there behind him in the bathroom. Could still picture how she looked in that shirt, in those shorts…

Choking back a groan, he closed his eyes briefly and gave his head a shake.

He knew they needed to split up, that he needed to get away from her. He should have figured out a way to convince her. He'd only been back for five minutes and he was already this much on edge. He didn't even want to think about how many hours lay ahead until dawn. He nearly groaned again at the thought.

Damn.

It was going to be a long night.

Chapter Five

As he often did on mornings when he was at the farm, Dick Bridges stood on the back balcony of his family home and surveyed the scene beyond. This location off his bedroom always offered a stirring view, the vast acreage of the Bridges homestead stretching into the horizon. The land had been in his family for generations, and seeing it always gave him a distinct sense of satisfaction, reminding him of who he was, where he had come from, the rich heritage to which be belonged.

Now, though, he focused his attention on the lawn directly below the balcony, thinking more of the future than the past. The lawn was empty now, the greenery lush and vibrant in the early morning sunlight. In three days, it would be filled with people who had come to hear his son announce his candidacy for president of this country. He could picture it clearly, as he had numerous times over the years. The mass of eager, smiling faces. The cheers and applause filling the air. The banners emblazoned with the name Richard Bridges. His son's name, as well as his own.

Once, when he'd imagined such a day, it was his own moment he had dreamed of—the smiling faces, the cheers and applause there for him alone. But when that day had come, the reality had fallen far short of the dream. The crowd had been disappointing, the cheers underwhelming. And he'd known before his campaign had even begun that he was going to lose. He wasn't going to be president of this great nation.

He could still taste the bitterness of that knowledge, and he frowned, his fingers tightening on the railing. He was familiar with what people thought of him, all the negatives that had been listed against him over the years. He was too cold. Too ambitious. Even when he tried to be pleasant and affable, there was a hardness to him he couldn't quite hide that turned people off. It was why his own political career had never advanced further than it had. His mouth curled in a sneer. Too many people acted as though they were electing someone to be their best friend, rather than a strong, qualified leader, the fools.

But this was going to be different. Everyone loved Rich, everyone knew Rich was going to win. The other side was having a difficult time finding a candidate to launch even a token opposition. No, when this Richard Bridges stood before that crowd, it was going to be a moment of victory before a single vote was cast. And Dick would be there, standing behind his son on the stage whose pieces were waiting below to be assembled, basking in that applause as though it were for him at last.

His smile returned, the warmth of that moment filling him as though it was happening right now. The relentless drive, the open ambition, that had been considered a weakness for his own career was exactly what had brought them all to the brink of success. When it had seemed that his son was too weak, when it had appeared the boy would ruin everything, it was he who had taken the necessary steps to ensure the future he'd dreamed of would come to fruition. He had no regrets about any of it. He'd done only what he'd had to. And his job wasn't done. As Rich's campaign manager, he would use that drive others had considered a negative to propel his son straight to the White House.

Determination hardening inside him, he thought of another day soon to come. Larger crowds. Greater applause. The crowning achievement of his life.

Rich's inauguration day. When Richard Bridges, the man Dick had given his own name for this very reason, would be sworn in as President of the United States.

Some might think it was premature to even imagine such a thing. After all, anything could happen in the next two years.

Dick knew better. Nothing would happen. He wouldn't let it. Just as he hadn't let it before.

Nothing could stop them now. Nothing would be allowed to.

Nothing.

THE FIRST THING AUDREY saw as they approached their destination was a sign on the outskirts of town declaring Welcome to Barrett's Mill, Hometown of U.S. Senator Richard Bridges. The sight of that name grabbed her attention and held it as they approached, the letters looming larger, seeming more and more like a threat, the closer they came to the sign. Despite her determination to come, she'd been increasingly uneasy all morning, and now they were finally here, the sight of that name driving it home.

No doubt about it. This was Bridges's domain. They were definitely headed straight into the heart of enemy territory.

She released a pent-up breath when they moved past the sign, but even having the words out of view didn't ease her tension.

No turning back now.

Fighting a shudder, she glanced over at Jason to see if he was similarly affected. There was no indication he was. He stared straight ahead, his expression stony.

He'd cut his hair before dyeing it, the same way she had. She'd offered to help him, even though the idea of any physical contact with him made her nervous as hell. The suggestion had made sense, especially given how long his hair had been. He'd still refused, and she hadn't known whether to be relieved or offended, the way he couldn't quite meet her eyes, telling her exactly why he'd turned down the offer.

He'd still done a good job of it. If she hadn't known he'd done it himself, she never would have guessed. The cut was more flattering than the long hair he'd had before, perfectly framing his strong profile and flawless features. With his hair dyed and the sunglasses in place, he did look sufficiently different from both the pictures she'd seen and the way he'd appeared earlier, hopefully enough to keep him from being recognized. But it was also still apparent that he was a very good-looking man. Staring at his face, she felt the same rush of attraction, her heart quickening, her body responding just as it had before.

Swallowing, she forced herself to look away and focus on the map in her hands.

"Do you know how to get to the first place on the list?" he asked.

"I think so." They'd downloaded a map of the town and a list of the motels and bed-and-breakfasts in the area, figuring their first item of business was to find a place to stay. Audrey doubted it was going to be easy. This was a relatively small community, and with Bridges holding his big campaign kickoff in just a few days, there likely wouldn't be many rooms available, if any.

She directed him toward the first address on the list, then looked out the window to keep track of their surroundings. Her tension only grew as they moved farther into town. Red-white-and-blue banners were draped on storefronts and buildings all along the main street, almost as if it were the Fourth of July rather than early March. Signs had been put up in seemingly every window.

Welcome Home, Richard Bridges!

Bridges for President!

Vote Bridges!

The whole town seemed ready to celebrate its favorite son. Audrey could understand why Bridges had chosen to launch his campaign here. This was the quintessential American small town. The main street was lined with old-fashioned buildings, occupied by what appeared to be local businesses, with no national companies in sight. The sidewalks were dotted with trees bursting with new leaves. The scene looked straight out of a movie set.

If she hadn't guessed it was going to be hard to find a room, the sight of the crowds on the sidewalks would have confirmed it. Seeing all the smiling faces, Audrey felt a pang of sadness. She could imagine how these people would react to learning the truth about Bridges. It wasn't easy finding out the truth about someone you respected. Many of them wouldn't want to hear it, which meant many of those smiling faces were potential enemies.

A wave of hopelessness rose within her. This seemed so impossible, but they simply had no other options.

As expected, the first two places they tried turned them away and suggested they wouldn't be able to find a room in town unless they got a local to rent one in a private home.

The third B and B on the list was a cozy three-story house on the corner of a quiet street. A hand-carved sign hanging between twin posts on the front lawn identified it as Marybeth's Inn. Audrey immediately reduced her hopes. A place this nice would surely have been booked up early on.

She and Jason still made their way to the front door. There was no one in sight when they stepped inside. Audrey moved to the small, unmanned reception desk and rang the bell on the counter. The simple chime echoed into the high ceiling and down the halls.

It took a few moments, but she finally heard footsteps approaching quickly in response to the bell. One set of feet padded down the staircase, and an attractive woman in her fifties appeared.

"Good morning," she said with a broad smile. "May I help you?"

"I certainly hope so," Jason said warmly, with a trace of weariness Audrey suspected he didn't have to feign at this point. "We're looking for a room for a few days and are really hoping you have one available."

The woman's smile instantly faded into a look of chagrin, just like the people at the first two places they'd stopped. "Oh, I'm sorry. We're all booked up. I'm afraid you'll find every place in town is, and likely the next town over, too."

"That's what we heard," Audrey said on a sigh. "We didn't realize that Richard Bridges is kicking off his presidential campaign here in a few days."

"Yes, it's all anyone can talk about around here. I'm surprised you didn't hear about it."

"We had no idea he was from here. Do you know him?"

The woman's expression tightened. "No," she said thinly. "I don't." Both her tone and her face said she didn't want to, either. Evidently, they'd managed to find the one person in town who wasn't a fan. Interesting. "If you didn't know about that, may I ask what brings you to Barrett's Mill?"

Knowing what was about to happen, Audrey braced herself, keeping her smile in place and trying not to tense.

Jason took her hand in his, clasping their fingers together tightly. It didn't matter that they were both wearing gloves to make his look less conspicuous. She still felt a jolt in her chest at the contact, even if they weren't skin to skin.

"We're newlyweds," Jason said. He glanced at Audrey and smiled. "On our honeymoon."

Audrey made herself smile back and gaze into his eyes. They couldn't present themselves as journalists.

With so many reporters in town, someone might wonder why they were here and who they were working for, and the last thing they needed was anyone looking at Jason too closely. If they claimed to be Bridges supporters, there for his announcement, they also might draw attention from a reporter wanting to interview people so enthusiastic about Bridges they'd come all this way. But in the middle of a major story, no one would pay much attention to a couple of hapless newlyweds.

Audrey understood the reasons, knew perfectly well this wasn't real. But as she looked into his eyes and smiled and felt his fingers wound through hers, what she felt inside her in response seemed entirely too real indeed.

She suddenly realized she had been standing there staring into Jason's eyes for far too long. She didn't have to fake the embarrassment that rose in her cheeks as she tore her gaze away, looking back at the woman with a self-conscious chuckle. "My great-aunt actually lived in Barrett's Mill as a child and always talked about how beautiful it was, so when we decided to elope, I talked Ben into coming here for the honeymoon. It never occurred to us that we'd have trouble finding a place to stay."

"What's your great-aunt's name? Maybe I remember her."

"Martha Greer," Audrey lied without missing a beat.

The woman seemed to consider the name before slowly shaking her head. "I'm afraid that doesn't sound familiar."

"I'm sure she must have been before your time,"

Audrey said. "Anyway, I'm sorry that we bothered you. You have such a lovely place. Thank you for your time though."

As she and Jason started to turn away, she held her breath, trying not to get her hopes up.

"Wait."

Audrey's hopes immediately shot up. When they turned back, the woman was gently biting her lip, apparently deep in thought. "I do have one room," the woman said hesitantly, after a moment. "It's in the basement though. It was my son's when he was a teenager, and we made a space for him that was out of the way of the guests, so he could have some privacy. I normally wouldn't think of renting it, but it does have its own bathroom, and if you give me an hour or so I'm sure I can get it fixed up real nice for you."

"That sounds wonderful," Jason said with a grin. "Somewhere with some privacy is just what we need. You're a lifesaver. By the way, I'm Ben Randall and this is my wife, Lila."

"Marybeth Kent," she introduced herself. "Good to meet you. I'm glad to be able to help. Honeymooners shouldn't have to worry about where they'll be spending the night. They should be enjoying themselves." She said the last with a sparkle in her blue eyes, before turning to move behind the front desk.

Taking in the woman's friendly smile, Audrey felt a twinge of guilt at having deceived such a kind woman. She did her best to shake off the feeling. Marybeth was being paid for a room she otherwise wouldn't be. If anything, they were doing her a favor.

Audrey couldn't help but wonder why Marybeth

hadn't rented out the room. Even if it wasn't one she normally would, with rooms in such high demand right now, she could have charged a premium for it. Yet she'd been willing to let it remain empty. Audrey suspected it wasn't a coincidence that someone who didn't appear to be a fan of Rich Bridges had let a room go unrented rather than offer it to another reporter or Bridges staffer.

She studied Marybeth's smiling face anew, wondering if the woman really disliked Richard Bridges that much and why.

The questions chased away the last of her guilt.

They may have had to lie to get the room, but Audrey had a feeling she and Jason were exactly where they needed to be.

REVIEWING THE ARCHIVES of the local newspaper had seemed like a good idea when Stone thought of it. If anything had happened involving Bridges the summer before he left for Europe, it may have made the local paper. It seemed like the best place for them to start, at any rate.

That was before he discovered that each year's issues were preserved on a single piece of film, then found himself crowded next to Audrey in front of a tiny cubicle containing a projector, trying to scan through the back issues from that summer at the same time.

They didn't both need to do it. One person was more than capable of handling it. But he hadn't wanted to risk missing out on anything, and he knew better than to think she would willingly leave it to him. It was only once they started that he realized he'd made a mistake. It didn't look like there was much to miss out on. As was to be expected, there wasn't exactly a lot of big news in a small town like this. The stories were a collection of slices of life that could only be interesting to the people involved, and were incredibly dull for anyone else.

Not to mention he was finding it impossible to concentrate on what he was supposed to when she was sitting so damn close.

He held himself stock-still, doing his best to avoid even brushing against her. It wasn't easy. Their two chairs were wedged together as tightly as possible, so they could both see. It also didn't really matter. He could still feel the heat of her body so strongly they might as well be pressed up against each other, could still smell her, the light, feminine scent filling his senses with every breath he took. God, did she have to smell so good, too?

He tried to focus on the words on the screen, only to realize he'd scanned the same passage several times without it sinking in.

"Look at this," she said, thankfully pulling his attention back to the matter at hand. Leaning forward, she raised her hand and tapped the screen.

Stone straightened in his seat, somehow managing not to brush against her. "What is it?"

"A mention of the Bridgeses. It's not much, but so far it's the only one I've seen."

"Something is better than nothing."

"And I think this definitely could be something. A young man who worked on the Bridges farm died in a car accident late that July. His name was Tim Raymer. It says he was apparently driving home from the farm late that night when his car went off the road and struck a tree. The car burst into flames and wasn't found until it was too late." She swallowed, and when she spoke again, it was quietly, her voice thick. "He burned to death inside."

His eyes had reached the words on the screen just as she said them. The double impact of seeing and hearing them hit him like bullets to the chest. He couldn't breathe, the air knocked from his lungs. The words he'd been reading vanished, replaced by an image that rose in his mind, so vivid he might as well be seeing it in front of him. A car in flames, burning before his very eyes. He no longer heard Audrey's voice. He only heard the screams, echoing endlessly in his ears.

Lisa. The girls. Burning to death before his very eyes.

He'd tried to get them out. He still remembered the heat of the flames, of the metal against his hands. He'd heard them screaming, knew he had to get them out. Later he wondered if he'd really heard what he thought he had, or whether it had been his own screams or those of his neighbors trying to pull him away. They may have been beyond screaming by then, already lost in the time it had taken him to react to the sound of the explosion and rush outside.

The feeling of something tugging on his hand finally broke through the emotions washing through him. Numbly, he looked down to see someone's fingers wrapped around his gloved ones. He followed the arm they were attached to all the way up to Audrey's face. She was looking at him, her eyes warm with concern and sympathy.

"Are you okay?" she whispered.

Anger sparked in his belly, piercing the numbness. He wanted to tell her no, to ask her what the hell kind of question that was. No, he wasn't okay. He hadn't been for more than two years, and likely never would again.

The flash of irrational anger died as he remembered exactly who he was looking at, realized that the sadness in her eyes wasn't just for him. Hal's home had been torched with him in it, so there was a good chance he'd burned to death, too, if he hadn't been dead already when the house had gone up.

"Yeah," he made himself say. He knew he should say something to her and return the comforting gesture, see how she was holding up in this. He couldn't make himself do it. That connection between them was too strong. He couldn't risk deepening it. Even now, her hand felt impossibly warm on his, even through the leather glove.

Looking away from the shared pain in her eyes, he turned his focus back to the screen. "I wonder if Bridges knew him, or vice versa."

He felt her gaze remain on him for a few moments before she finally glanced back at the article. "Well, according to this, Tim Raymer was seventeen, so roughly the same age as Bridges. There's a chance they knew each other."

"It certainly sounds possible. It's hard to believe there's much to do around here, and knowing how much Bridges loved horses even back then, it makes sense that he would know someone his own age who worked on the farm."

"Even so, there's no reason to believe this has anything to do with Bridges's secret," she admitted.

"Maybe not, but it's all we have to go on at the moment, and we have to start somewhere. Besides, we need to talk to anyone who knew Bridges back then, see if they can tell us more about him. Tim's obviously not around, but his parents might be, and they could tell us if Tim talked about Bridges, or point us in the direction of anyone else who worked at the farm at the same time."

"It says here Tim lived with his uncle, Clint Raymer. There's no mention of his parents."

"It's worth a shot," he said. "It looks like we have a few weeks left to go through, but so far I haven't seen anything else here that seems relevant."

"Neither have I," Audrey agreed. "Okay, so we'll start with Clint Raymer. Let's see if we can track him down."

After printing out the article for future reference, they scanned the rest of the issues for any follow-up stories. There weren't any. Neither Tim Raymer nor the Bridges family were mentioned again in the paper during the rest of the summer or the months immediately following.

They returned the film to the librarian and obtained a copy of the local phone book. A "C. Raymer" was listed, but no address was given. Audrey wrote down the number, and they returned to the librarian, a woman who appeared to be in her early thirties.

"Excuse me," Jason said, drawing her attention. "We're trying to find a Clint Raymer. Is there any chance you know where he lives?"

The woman simply blinked at them, her expression going slack with surprise. "Clint Raymer?"

"That's right. Do you know him?" he asked, even though it was clear from her reaction she did.

The woman nodded slowly. "Sure. Why are you looking for him, if you don't mind my asking?"

"For my great-aunt," Audrey said before he could improvise a cover story, surprising him. "He's a distant cousin of hers, one of the few relatives she has left in the world, and we told her we'd try to look him up while we're in the area. She hasn't spoken to him in years, and she'd like to get back in touch."

The librarian's eyebrows raised slightly. "Oh, I didn't know Clint had any family left. That's nice. He could probably use some."

"What do you mean?" Jason asked.

The woman bit her lip, and he sensed her choosing her words carefully. "Exactly how much do you know about Clint?"

"Not much at all," Audrey admitted.

The woman grimaced, then lowered her voice. "Clint has a bit of a…drinking problem, and even when he's not drinking he's not always the nicest person to be around. Like I said, it might be nice for him to have some family. I'm just not sure how nice it would be for you or your aunt."

"I understand," Audrey said. "My aunt was afraid that might be the case. Thank you for the warning. Maybe a visit from family will do him good. Can you tell us where he lives?"

After a moment's hesitation, the woman reached for a pencil and a piece of paper. "His house is outside of town. It's the only one on that road, so you shouldn't have any trouble finding it. The hard part is finding the road, but I can draw you a map."

"Thank you," Audrey said warmly. "That's really kind of you."

The woman grimaced again, her expression clearly saying she wondered if Audrey would feel the same way once she met Clint Raymer.

Two minutes later, they headed out of the library, the map neatly folded in Audrey's bag. As they approached the exit, Stone slipped his sunglasses back on. Stepping out of the building, he immediately scanned the surrounding area.

A familiar face jumped out at him in the crowd.

It was the man from the diner.

Shock jolted through him, but Jason didn't let it stop him. The man wasn't looking in their direction and didn't appear to have noticed them. Jason spun away from the man, grabbing Audrey's arm and propelling her in the other direction as well.

"What's going on?" she asked under her breath.

"Trouble. Our friend is here."

She inhaled sharply but didn't comment or question him further. He was glad for that. They didn't have time. They had to get out of here.

The sidewalk was still crowded, and most of the people around them didn't seem to be in any particular hurry. Not that the two of them could rush anyway. The worst thing they could do was draw attention to themselves. They needed to blend seamlessly into the crowd. So Stone matched his pace to that of the people around them, no matter how much every instinct wanted to go faster. Beside him, Audrey did the same.

It didn't seem likely the man would try something in public on a busy street. Even if he had a gun with a silencer, he wasn't going to open fire in front of all these people. No, Jason's main concern was having the man spot them at all.

Though his car was parked not too far up ahead, they couldn't go to it, couldn't risk the man identifying it as theirs if he saw them enter it. Nor could they stay together, he realized. The man was probably looking for two people instead of one, and even with their hair changed, they were still the same approximate heights and shapes. Staying together was too much of a risk, even if the last thing he wanted to do was let her go.

He still forced his fingers to loosen on her arm, leaning closer as he did it. "Make your way to the next block and turn left," he said under his breath. "I'll meet you there. If anything happens, run."

He sensed her stiffen in surprise and saw her shoot a startled glance at him out of the corner of his eye. He didn't acknowledge her reaction. As soon as the words were out of his mouth, he shifted away from her, slowing slightly. After a moment, she gradually picked up speed, not enough to be noticeable, but enough that she moved in front of him.

Stone made a conscious effort to shift his head slightly from side to side, not so much that anyone behind him would be able to see his profile, but so that it appeared he was looking around himself. All the while, he kept his eyes on Audrey's back, entirely too aware of the tension crawling up his own. Whether it was from someone's eyes on him or the simple knowledge that there could be, he didn't know. He could only keep moving forward, only hope the man hadn't seen them.

Audrey finally reached the corner and slipped around it. Her hair fell over her face, keeping it from view as she turned. Stone was still several yards back. He slid over to that side of the sidewalk to follow.

An eternity later, he finally made it there. As he rounded the corner, he risked a glance back.

The man wasn't following them. Jason didn't see his face in the crowd. He was nowhere in sight.

The tightness in Jason's chest didn't ease. The man could appear again at any moment. He focused his attention in front of him, automatically seeking Audrey.

"Jason," she said softly, stepping forward from the side where she'd moved out of the way.

He motioned her forward. "Come on."

She fell back into step beside him. They quickly made their way back to the car, neither speaking until they were both inside. As he started the engine and pulled away from the curb, he kept his eyes on his mirrors, scanning for any sign of the man.

"How did he manage to track us here already?" Audrey asked quietly, as though there was still a risk of anyone overhearing. "Do you think someone identified us?"

"No, even if someone did, it's unlikely he could have gotten here this fast." Still keeping an eye on the street, Stone pulled into traffic. "The book," he said finally. "If he figured out that we really don't know what's in it, then it would make sense that we would try to re-create Hal's investigation to find out on our own. He has an advantage on us, because he probably has a copy of the book, so he knows what Hal uncovered. Whatever it is has to be connected to Barrett's Mill, so he came here expecting us to."

"Well, at least we know we're on the right track," Audrey said grimly.

That was the one positive about the man's appearance here, Jason agreed silently. Unfortunately, everything else about it was bad.

They didn't just have to avoid any of his former colleagues or any members of Bridges's staff who might know about them. They had to avoid the assassin who was specifically looking for them. In a town this small, it hardly seemed possible.

The man was already closing in on them.

And they were running out of time.

Chapter Six

Shaw kept a smile on his lips as he stepped into the library, part of the pleasant expression necessary to blend and go unnoticed. As he took in the racks of books before him, he nearly shook his head. He hadn't spent this much time around books since he was a kid back in school. Back then, he'd never wanted much to do with them. Now it seemed he couldn't get away from them.

He'd spent half the night reading Talmadge's book. The man had been a hell of a writer, Shaw had to give him that. Shaw had only been in it for the information, but the book had been a better read than he'd expected.

Too bad Talmadge had also been a hell of a reporter, which was exactly why he'd had to die.

He'd found out something, all right. Specifically, one thing that could have proven very messy if it had been allowed to get out.

Which it still might. That was why Shaw was here.

Bridges had been shocked by what Shaw had told him was in the book, and ordered him to contain the situation, exactly as Shaw had known he would and had already been planning to do.

If Stone and Ellison were in Barrett's Mill, he'd find them eventually. In the meantime, he had a few other loose ends to deal with.

If they did come here, they would no doubt try to talk to certain people, some of whom would be more than willing to talk to them, if Talmadge's book was any indication. Which meant he had to make sure those people couldn't talk to Stone and Ellison.

Or to anyone else.

Spotting the reference desk up ahead, he moved toward it. He had sources who could have given him the information he needed, but there was no use paying for something he could get free. Not to mention doing a little legwork offered the opportunity to get a feel for the town.

Walking down Main Street had given him a good sense of what he needed to know. This was a small town, which had both advantages and disadvantages. In a town this size, people tended to notice strangers. Lucky for him, plenty of strangers were in town, which would make it easier for him not to stand out. On the downside, there were plenty of potential witnesses squeezed into a fairly small area. He was still going to have to proceed carefully.

But first he needed another book.

He came to a stop in front of the reference desk. A librarian—mid-thirties, short brown hair—stood behind it, her head down as she focused on some kind of paperwork.

"Excuse me," he said politely.

The librarian looked up and blinked at him, her lips

quickly curving in a smile. "Oh, I'm sorry. May I help you?"

"I hope so," he said pleasantly, matching her smile. "You wouldn't happen to have a local phone book available, would you?"

"Do YOU THINK it's even safe to go see Clint Raymer?" Audrey asked as they followed the map the librarian had drawn for them. "If he does know something, then Hal might have spoken to him and mentioned him in the book. If so, that man could figure out we'd go to see him."

"In that case, that man could be after Raymer anyway, which means we have to get to him first."

Jason was right, she acknowledged with a frown. While it was a risk, it was a necessary one. If Clint knew something, they needed to find out what it was, even if it meant giving their pursuer a chance to catch up when they'd only just escaped him.

A tremor of apprehension slid through her, raising goose bumps on her skin. There were too many choices facing them, decisions that had to be made quickly and correctly, with no room for error. The stakes were too high. One misstep and it could mean their lives.

Of course, ever since she'd met him, Jason had had no trouble making fast decisions, and he had yet to step wrong. From the first time he'd saved her life to the escape from the diner, he seemed to have a knack for knowing exactly what to do. Back on the street, he'd seen their pursuer and quickly devised a plan, albeit one she hadn't agreed with. She'd immediately understood what he was doing, giving her a chance to get away while keeping himself a target. He'd even told her to run if anything happened. She'd wanted to argue, but naturally there hadn't been any way she could at that moment. Fortunately, they'd both gotten away in the end.

The moment had reminded her of something that she'd known from the start, from that first conversation at the bar when he'd refused to get involved and she'd looked into the bleakness of his eyes.

"You have to know they're going to come after you."

"Why should I care?"

In the end, he'd chosen to get involved after all, but she knew it wasn't because he was just as much of a target and he wanted to save his own life. He'd only gotten involved to save hers.

Some people might think that was noble, that he was willing to put his life on the line for hers. But it was only noble when someone was risking something that mattered to him, and she didn't believe his life did.

He didn't think he had anything left to live for.

Sadness welling up inside her, she eyed him curiously. She wanted to believe she was wrong. There was only one reason to believe she was, a question that had been nagging at her since that first meeting.

"That was some impressive quick thinking back there," Audrey said, trying to keep her tone casual. "You're pretty good at evading people."

"It's something I've picked up over the years."

"You don't have to tell me. I remember how hard it was to track you down."

"Obviously not hard enough," he pointed out dryly.

"I suppose not. There's just one thing I don't understand. When I tracked you down yesterday and told you someone was probably coming after you, you acted like you didn't care, like it didn't matter to you whether you live or die. And yet you live completely off the grid, making it as difficult as possible for anyone to find you, like you expect someone to come after you and you're doing everything to make sure they can't. Doesn't quite compute, for someone who doesn't care if they live or die. Do you think they're still coming after you? The people who killed your family?"

He shook his head. "I know they're not. There's no one left to hold a grudge."

"So why go to all that trouble?"

"I just want to be left alone."

Her heart sank. "Then it has nothing to do with survival."

"What are you getting at?"

She hardened her tone. "I want you to know that I don't expect you to sacrifice yourself for me, and I don't want you to. Whether or not you think so, your life is just as important as mine."

He snorted. "Is that why you were so insistent on not letting me come to Barrett's Mill by myself? Because you weren't sure if I care whether I live or die?"

"I told you why I wanted to come, and everything I said was true. But I admit I did wonder."

He didn't say anything, staring straight ahead, his expression hard and emotionless.

When the silence became more than she could stand, she asked quietly, "*Do* you? Do you care?"

He remained silent, which she was afraid was answer enough.

Before she could think of anything else to say, he jerked his head toward the road in front of them. "I think this is it."

Even as he said it, the vehicle began to slow. Audrey looked up in surprise to see they were outside of town. He was pulling off onto a side road.

She could have pressed the question, but she suspected there wasn't much of a point.

As Jason maneuvered the car down the road, Audrey surveyed the dense trees lining it on both sides. They almost seemed to create a tunnel around the roadway. Looking ahead, she could see nothing but the trees, and more road stretching ahead.

She wondered if Tim Raymer had died somewhere along this stretch of road. If that was the case, she could understand why he might not have been discovered until it was too late. Even after a good thirty seconds of traveling down the road, the house remained out of sight. Any accident that happened here would likely not be visible from whatever lay at the end of the road, and probably wouldn't be heard either.

The trees finally cleared, revealing a one-story house set on a small plot of land. The house and the garage beside it were both old and ill-kept, with fading paint and missing shingles on the roofs. The grass was patchy and choked with weeds. Everything about the scene spoke of neglect and decay.

An ancient blue pickup truck was parked in front of the house. Stone pulled up behind it. "I hope that means he's home."

Climbing out of the car, they moved to the front door. A rusty screen door hung in front of it. There didn't appear to be a doorbell. Audrey had no other options but to knock directly on the metal of the screen door. She rapped on it quickly, wincing at the way it rattled in the frame.

A minute passed. No response.

"What if that man was already here?" she murmured. "What if something happened to Clint Raymer?"

"Then we at least need to find out," he said.

Nodding grimly, Audrey knocked again, louder this time.

Still nothing.

Her tension growing, she leaned over to try to see through the front window. The curtains were closed and they were heavy enough that there was no way to see through them.

She knocked again. "Do you think we should try the door?"

Jason opened his mouth to respond when the front door was suddenly wrenched open. An angry face pressed up against the screen, glaring at them through red-rimmed, bloodshot eyes.

"What the hell do you want?"

The man was in his seventies at the very least, his face bloated and mottled from what Audrey suspected was years of alcohol abuse. Considering the trouble he seemed to be having focusing his eyes, she would guess he'd had more than a little to drink already today. It seemed a good bet that this was the man they were looking for. "Mr. Raymer?"

"Who's asking?"

"We were hoping to speak with you about your nephew."

"Don't got one."

"You didn't have a nephew named Tim Raymer?"

"I did. Don't anymore. He's dead."

"We know. We'd still like to speak with you about him."

The man's bleary eyes narrowed on Audrey for a long moment. "Eh, why the hell not? I ain't got nothing better to do."

He turned around and walked into the house without opening the screen door for them. Audrey and Jason exchanged a confused glance. With a shrug, Jason opened the screen door and held it for her. After a moment, Audrey stepped inside. She supposed it had been an invitation, or at least as much of one as they were going to get.

Clint Raymer had already plopped himself in a well-worn recliner in the dingy, poorly lit living room, a beer can clutched in his right hand. Audrey did her best to keep her distaste from showing. Even if he'd offered, she would have hesitated to take a seat herself. The room was a mess. Empty beer bottles and unwashed dishes crowded the coffee table. Piles of dirty clothes and newspapers were everywhere. A few odors she didn't even want to try to identify reached her nose.

Clint didn't say anything, simply watching them through hooded eyes as they stepped into the middle of the room before him.

"Did your nephew live here with you?" Jason asked.

"Yep," the man grunted. "Ever since I got stuck with him."

"How did he come to live with you?" Audrey asked.

"His ma up and died. She was my sister. Wasn't nobody else."

"What about his father?"

"Never knew who he was. His ma never said." The last words came out on a sneer that oozed contempt, whether for his sister or his nephew, Audrey couldn't tell. Either way, it wasn't exactly a nice attitude to have toward his own family. She tried not to frown and show her disapproval, even as she felt a twinge of sympathy for Tim Raymer, stuck in this awful house with this awful man. She had a feeling neither had been much better thirty-five to forty years ago.

"It doesn't sound like you were too happy to have your nephew living with you," Jason noted.

"Eh, he was all right when he was a kid. It was good to have somebody to do chores around here, clean up, cook. I never got hitched myself, so never had a wife to do that stuff. But as he grew up, he got too big for his britches. Thought he was real smart, too good for this town, better than me. Kept saying he was going to college, make something of himself, not waste his life like me. Who's going to pay for this *college,* I ask him. He didn't have an answer for that. Guess he wasn't so smart after all."

"He was working at the Bridges farm the summer he died, is that right?" Jason asked.

"That's right. Just like his mama used to." His eyes narrowed, sparkling with a sudden unexpected shrewdness. "That why you're here? Bridges?" The way he said it, he was wholly unimpressed by the town's favorite son.

"Yes," Audrey said. "Did your nephew talk to you about his job there?" she asked, even as she had the feeling Tim Raymer wouldn't have wanted to talk to his uncle about much of anything. "Do you know if he knew Rich Bridges?"

Clint smirked. "You're not really here about the boy, are you? You're here about the *girl*."

Audrey and Jason exchanged a glance. She could see he didn't have any more of an idea what the man was talking about than she did. "What girl?" Audrey asked.

"Timmy's girlfriend, Julie Ann Foster." The name came out on another sneer, and Audrey was almost surprised he didn't spit after saying it. "I told that writer all about her. Guess he finally got the word out in his book, huh?"

Excitement surged through her. So they were on the right track. "This writer. Was his name Hal Talmadge?"

Clint shrugged. "Sounds about right, I guess."

"I'm afraid he died recently. His book was lost. Would you be willing to tell us what you told him?"

"Sure. Somebody ought to get the truth out."

"So this Julie Ann Foster was your nephew's girlfriend?" Jason asked.

"She was till that summer. Looks like she dropped him just as soon as a bigger fish came along. Hell, maybe she used him to meet the big fish, same way she was trying to use him to get out of this town. Pretty girl, but she was nothing but trash, just like her folks.

She wanted to get out of here just like Timmy, and she figured he was her ticket to do it. At least until she found a surer thing." He raised his beer can in acknowledgment. "Well, she pulled it off, I'll give her that much."

"I'm sorry, Mr. Raymer," Jason said. "I don't follow."

The man took a long swallow from his can, studying them over the rim. "Huh," he said finally, lowering the can. "Guess you really don't know." He smacked his lips and smiled smugly. "Julie Ann changed her name. Calls herself Julia now. Fancy, huh? Julia Bridges. She's good ol' Rich Bridges's wife."

Stunned, Audrey could only stare at the man. "Your nephew's girlfriend later married Richard Bridges?" Jason asked, and she could tell from his tone he was just as surprised as she was. "Did you know she was seeing him at the time?"

"Not then, no. I only figured it out like most people, when he came back the next year and married her."

"Isn't it possible they didn't get together until that next summer?" she suggested.

"No. They got married too fast. Little Richie Bridges had barely come back to town when he and Julie Ann ran off and eloped. I heard old Dick was pissed. Hard to blame him. Can't imagine trash like her was what he had in mind for his golden boy. Ain't no way they knew each other long enough to want to get married. They must have been going out the summer before. I just should have put it together sooner. Rumor had it little Richie Bridges was seeing a local girl the summer Tim died. He was seen parking with some girl one time, but no one could see who she was. And Julie Ann used to go out to the farm—to 'visit' Tim, they said." He snorted. "More like to get her hooks in the Bridges kid."

"And then Tim died," Audrey concluded.

"Nice and easylike for Julie Ann, huh? She didn't even have to break up with him. Richie left town right after that. I figure Dick sent him packing to keep her away from him. Didn't work out the way he wanted, now did it?"

Was this the reason for Rich Bridges's sudden departure for Europe? Could it have been nothing more than Dick's attempt to break up a teenage romance? If so, then Raymer was right. It hadn't turned out as Dick had intended.

Clint shook his head slowly. "Don't say much for Richie Bridges now, does it? Fooling around with another fella's girl? Everybody thinks he's so damn perfect, but he ain't. Just another rich bastard taking what he wants. Not that Julie Ann made it all that hard for him, I bet."

"Are you sure Rich even knew she and Tim were dating?" Jason asked.

"He had to. You think she could go out there to the farm, where both of them were, and get away with one of them not knowing she was seeing the other?"

Audrey considered the man's words. If this was true, it did make the way Rich and Julia Bridges first met seem a little tawdry. It might be a little embarrassing for them, but she couldn't imagine Hal thinking it was enough to base his book on.

An honorable man…

Hal's title implied that Richard Bridges was anything but. Even so, a teenage love triangle was hardly the stuff of major scandals. Few people would hold something like that against Bridges, or even care. It might even make him seem more human, not the perfect person he often came across as. If anything, it might tarnish Julia Bridges's reputation more than her husband's.

Unless there was more to it, she thought, turning the facts over in her head.

Two young men, both involved with one young woman. One of the young men dies suddenly in a tragic accident, the other abruptly leaves the country, abandoning his established plans to attend college in the fall.

Unless, Audrey thought with a growing sense of foreboding, what seemed to be a tragic accident was something else altogether.

Chapter Seven

Howard Foley stared at the milk carton he'd just pulled out of the refrigerator and swallowed a sigh. He'd recognized something was wrong as soon as he'd picked up the carton. He didn't even have to look to know it.

The carton was empty.

It was a bad habit of his, placing an empty milk carton back in the refrigerator without thinking about it, too preoccupied with whatever else was on his mind to register what he was doing. Carol had tried to break him of the habit—or at least had done enough complaining about it—for most of the forty years they'd been married. But Carol had passed over a year ago, and now the only person left to care about empty milk cartons in the fridge was Howard himself, the sole victim of his own transgression.

Grimacing, he closed the refrigerator door and set the carton on the countertop. The sound it made as it hit the surface, a kind of echoing emptiness, was familiar. The whole house seemed filled with it. There'd been a time when he and Carol had thought that this house might be too small for their family, the two of them and their three children. Now Carol was gone, the children were grown and off to their own lives far from here, and the house seemed huge, so much empty space, with only him to amble around in it.

The worst part was that he couldn't even go into town to buy more milk. He wasn't leaving the house for the next few days. Barrett's Mill was full of Bridges supporters, all here for Rich Bridges's announcement that he was going to run for president. The mere thought of it made Howard's grimace deepen into an all-out scowl.

All those people, all those smiling faces. All for a man who didn't deserve any of it.

But they'd know the truth soon enough.

He felt a twinge of regret at the knowledge that a lot of people were going to be upset, disillusioned, and he'd played a part in that. But they needed to know the truth about the man before it was too late.

Bracing his hands on the kitchen sink, Howard tried to strengthen the rest of him in much the same way. The day was a long time coming, and the closer it came, the more nervous he became. Not about Bridges's actions being revealed, but his own complicity in them, even if no public reaction could compare to the guilt he'd carried all this time.

In the more than thirty-five years he'd served as the local medical examiner, he tried to do his best to serve the dead, to give them the dignity and respect they deserved. He had just one regret in his career, the sole deceased individual he'd failed to serve.

He'd been only thirty-two, new on the job, with a wife and—at the time—two young children to support. When he'd first seen the body, cause of death had seemed obvious. At least until he'd completed the autopsy and discovered otherwise.

He'd naturally taken his findings to the police chief, only to be informed that Dick Bridges wanted the case closed with a minimum of fuss, and that was exactly what was going to happen. It was going to be determined that the deceased died as a result of the fire caused when his car struck a tree. An unfortunate accident. Case closed.

Being fairly new to the area, Howard hadn't understood how Bridges could influence an investigation like that. The police chief had quickly set him straight. If Howard wanted to keep his job, he'd figure out fast how things worked around here and keep his mouth shut.

He did want to keep the job. It was a much-needed supplement to his burgeoning medical practice. He'd already known that the deceased had next to no family, only a deadbeat uncle who'd barely cared about the deceased at all. There was no one who really needed or deserved to have the truth told. No one but the victim himself.

So Howard had kept his mouth shut as ordered—even if doing so had never sat right with him—and kept his job. But he hadn't been able to completely bury the truth behind the lies he'd been ordered to tell. So he retained a copy of the true report, thinking that someday the time would come when he would be able to reveal the truth.

That day had arrived just less than a year ago, when a man had come to his door asking about an old case, wondering if he remembered.

As if he could forget.

Tim Raymer. A name that had never managed to fade into the past like so many others. A name he could have supplied before the stranger at his door said a single word, the sight of him alone giving Howard a premonition that told him exactly why the man had come. The time had finally arrived to tell the truth.

For almost a year, he'd waited for the day when the stranger would reveal the truth to the whole world. Now that Richard Bridges was about to officially announce his candidacy, that day was closer than ever. Everything that had been done would be revealed—including Howard's own role in the cover-up. He was prepared to face his own disgrace for the sake of the larger truth. The only small comfort of Carol's passing was that she wasn't here to see it.

The doorbell rang, the sound jarring him out of his thoughts. Howard raised his head and looked back toward the front door. He couldn't imagine who it might be. He wasn't expecting anyone. Most of his days passed in solitude. Still, grateful for the distraction, he made his way to the front door.

He didn't move as fast as he used to, and whoever it was rang the bell a second time before he reached the door. "I'm coming, I'm coming," he muttered.

It never occurred to him to ask who it was. This was a small town. Innocent. So as he reached for the knob, he didn't give a thought to opening the door.

At least until he did. And then it was too late.

Because just as he'd had a premonition when a man had appeared on his doorstep a year earlier, he knew as soon as he looked at this man that he shouldn't have opened the door.

"So what'd you think of Clint's story?" Audrey asked as they drove away from Raymer's house. "Could there be something there?"

"If so, it has to be more than Rich stealing another kid's girlfriend," Jason said.

"Like maybe there was more to Tim Raymer's death than just a tragic accident?"

He nodded. "Looks like we're on the same page then. But if that is the case, we're going to need a lot more to prove it. All we have so far is innuendo from the mouth of a drunk."

"True. The basic facts should be easy enough to confirm. When Rich left for Europe, when he and Julia married and whether she used to be known as Julie Ann Foster. And I'm sure if she did date Tim Raymer, others will remember, maybe people they went to school with."

"Marybeth appears to be roughly the same age as Rich and Julia Bridges," Jason pointed out. "She may have known Julia back then."

"We should ask her," Audrey agreed, remembering how she'd sensed that Marybeth didn't like Rich Bridges. Audrey wondered how she felt about his wife. "Well, if there is more to Tim Raymer's death, and Rich was involved, it could explain some things. Assuming what Clint told us is true, then maybe Rich didn't suddenly leave the country because his father was trying to put an end to his relationship with Julia. Maybe Dick was trying to keep him out of the reach of the law, in case anyone figured out what really happened to Tim. When they realized the crime had effectively been ruled an accident and Rich had escaped suspicion, he was free to return."

"It certainly makes more sense than Dick simply letting Rich postpone college to bum around Europe, or sending him overseas to stop the relationship," Jason noted.

"It could also explain why Rich suddenly fell in line with his father's plans for him."

"If Rich had something to do with Tim's death and Dick helped him cover it up, then Rich would have owed him. I wouldn't put it past Dick to hold it over his son's head to force him to do what he wanted."

"Well, if Clint is telling the truth, it sounds like Dick didn't have complete control over Rich's actions. He came back and married Julia anyway. Of course, that was only an act of rebellion, if Julia was as beneath his class as Clint made her out to be and Dick really disliked her." She glanced at him. "How much do you know about Julia Bridges?"

Jason frowned, his brow furrowing. "Nothing really. I never knew all that much about the Bridgeses' marriage. I don't even know what, if anything, she does for a living. She pretty much always seemed like the typical politician's spouse, supporting her husband while staying out of the limelight and not drawing too much attention to herself."

"Well, Hal's book was about Bridges's entire life, especially the parts that hadn't been explored much. It would make sense that the Bridgeses' marriage would come up."

"We definitely should learn more about Julia Bridges.

It could give us an idea of just how much of Clint Raymer's story we should believe."

"Sounds like a plan."

"On the other hand," he said after a moment, "it could be that none of this is important at all. Just because Hal spoke with him doesn't mean he found what Clint Raymer had to say useful. It was just gossip. Not to mention our tail never did show up, which could indicate Clint wasn't mentioned in the book, or if so, what he had to say wasn't a major part of what Hal wrote about."

He had a point, but her instincts told her they were on to something with the man's story. They'd warned Clint to be careful whom he talked to and to watch his back, that Bridges might not like what he had to say. Audrey had had the distinct feeling he hadn't taken their comments seriously. But then, Jason was right. What the man had to say really was unsubstantiated gossip. Even if it was relevant, Bridges might not consider an old drunk enough of a threat to need to be silenced. Audrey could only hope the latter was the case.

A few minutes later they arrived back at the inn. Walking inside, they found Marybeth at the front desk, speaking to a man standing on the other side of it. She noticed them as soon as they came through the door, looking up with a smile. "You're back!"

Audrey felt another twinge of guilt at how they'd deceived the woman, but managed to match her smile. "I hope it's not too soon."

"Not at all," Marybeth replied, coming around the desk. "I have the room ready for you. I think you'll be pleased with how it turned out."

"I'm sure we will be," Jason said, the warmth in his

voice nearly sending a shudder down Audrey's spine. When he turned on the charm like that, he sounded so different from the way he usually did—so smooth, so undeniably sexy. Even knowing it was feigned, she couldn't help but be affected by it.

As Audrey tried to shake off the feeling, the man Marybeth had been speaking to turned to face them. "You must be the folks who talked my mother into finally putting my old room to some use."

"This is my son, Will," Marybeth said, her pride obvious in both her voice and the way she looked up at him.

"Will Kent," the man said, extending his hand. He was a tall, handsome man in his thirties, with deep brown eyes and a broad smile. Everything about him exuded an easy friendliness. He was clearly Marybeth's son, the resemblance unmistakable even before she'd introduced him. "Good to meet you."

"Ben Randall," Jason said. "This is my wife, Lila. I hope you don't mind us using your room."

Amusement sparkled in the man's brown eyes. "It hasn't been my room for well over a decade now. It's long past time my mother took down the shrine."

"It was hardly that," Marybeth said with an indulgent grin. "Will's also our town mayor," she told Jason and Audrey.

"I'm also running for the state senate in the fall, if you happen to be from the area," he said smoothly.

"We're not, I'm afraid," Audrey said.

"Not a problem." He grinned. "Never hurts to ask. It's still good to meet you."

Audrey couldn't help but laugh. The man was a

charmer, she had to give him that. A lot of politicians came off as smarmy and insincere, but he clearly had natural charisma to spare. Given her current circumstances, she should be feeling skeptical toward anyone remotely connected with politics. Instead, she couldn't help but like him. Even without knowing anything about his positions, she had no trouble believing he could go far.

"I guess maybe someday Bridges won't be the only famous name in politics from Barrett's Mill," she said. "Do you know Rich Bridges?"

"I've never met him," Will said. "Though I'd like to. It's certainly inspiring to see how far somebody from our little town can go. Is that what made you decide to spend your honeymoon here?"

"Actually, we didn't even know about any of that," Audrey replied without so much as blinking. "My great-aunt grew up in the area before moving away. She always said how beautiful it was, so I convinced Ben to come here for our honeymoon and maybe reconnect with some distant relatives."

"Anybody we can help you find?" Marybeth asked.

"Actually, we spoke to someone this afternoon. Clint Raymer?"

Will and Marybeth both appeared as surprised as the librarian in town had. "I didn't know Clint had any family," Marybeth said carefully.

"Yes, well, I believe there was some kind of…difficulty between him and Aunt Martha's side of the family," Audrey said, as though she was being tactful. "They'd been out of touch for so long, and I thought I'd see if there was any way of broaching a reconciliation."

"Any luck?" Will asked.

"I'm not sure yet. I guess we'll see." Audrey glanced at Marybeth. "By any chance did you know *Tim* Raymer?"

Marybeth's eyebrows shot up. "Whew. Now there's a name I haven't heard in a long time. Sure I knew Tim. We were in the same grade all through school. He passed…must be thirty-five years ago now."

"What can you tell us about him?" Audrey asked, trying not to appear too eager. "Aunt Martha was sorry she didn't know him better."

"Oh, Tim was a nice fellow," Marybeth said genuinely enough that Audrey knew she wasn't just being polite. "He didn't have the easiest time of it, I'm afraid. You may know his mama passed when he was just a boy, and I don't think he ever knew his father. And, well, if you've met Clint, you can probably guess he wasn't all that interested in raising the boy. But Tim was smart, a hard worker. Everybody liked him. We all thought he'd go places. It's such a shame he died so young."

"Funny coincidence," Jason said smoothly. "Clint mentioned that Tim used to date Richard Bridges's wife before he married her. I guess she was known as Julie Ann Foster back then?"

Audrey watched Marybeth's reaction closely. She wasn't disappointed. The woman went pale, her jaw tightening. "I believe he may be right. I'd forgotten about that. It was so long ago."

"You must have known her, too," Audrey noted.

"Not really," Marybeth said thinly. "We weren't part of the same crowd." She shook her head as though to clear it. "Anyway, you must be wanting to get settled in. Let me show you to your room."

Once again wondering about Marybeth's reaction, Audrey nodded. "That would be great."

"Can I help you with your bags?" Will asked, stepping forward.

Shaking his head, Jason picked up the two bags he'd brought in from the car and set at his feet when they'd entered. "That's okay. We're traveling pretty light. Thanks though."

"Well, nice meeting you folks," Will said.

Jason and Audrey returned the sentiment, turning to follow Marybeth.

She led them to a back staircase and down a carpeted set of stairs. At the bottom landing were two doors, one leading left, the other right. Pulling out a key, Marybeth unlocked and opened the door on the left, then stepped inside, flipping on the light.

Audrey followed her in. She saw immediately, her heart sinking, that Marybeth had gone out of her way to make the room suitable for a honeymoon. If Will Kent hadn't been exaggerating and Marybeth had been keeping the room as any kind of shrine, there were no signs of it left. No personal items were in view. Instead, a variety of big and small candles had been placed on the top of the dresser and on the bedside tables. A few vases filled with what appeared to be fresh flowers were placed around the space. Even without those touches, it was a nice room, the dark blue carpet clean and thick, the walls painted a warm cream color, the furniture in flawless condition. From where she stood, Audrey could see the adjoining bathroom Marybeth had promised.

If they hadn't just come down the stairs, Audrey might not have guessed this was a basement room. Other than having windows while this room did not, she couldn't imagine any of the upstairs rooms being much nicer than this. It only increased Audrey's suspicion that Marybeth could very well have rented this room long before they arrived if she'd wanted to.

Finally unable to avoid it, Audrey's attention went to the bed. She might have expected it to be too small to fit two people since Will Kent had slept here as a teenager, but the mattress appeared to be at least queen-size. Clearly, the bed could accommodate two people, and had obviously been prepped to do just that, the comforter already turned down, plush white pillows propped invitingly against the headboard.

Not that it was going to, of course.

One of them could easily take the floor. Audrey didn't really care which one of them did, as long as someone did.

Not that they could let Marybeth know that. She had to expect them to hop in bed as soon as she left.

Audrey barely managed to suppress a shudder at the thought—or the images that suddenly filled her head.

Summoning a smile, Audrey turned to the woman who was clearly waiting for a reaction. "It's perfect. Thank you so much."

Marybeth beamed at her, a knowing gleam sparkling in her blue eyes. "Well, I'll leave you two to settle in. Let me know if you need anything. I'm right upstairs."

"Thanks again," Audrey said sincerely.

Handing Jason the key, Marybeth backed out of the room, closing the door behind her.

Releasing a breath, Audrey finally looked at him. As usual, his expression betrayed none of his feelings. Or maybe there were no feelings to betray because he wasn't as affected by the implications of this room as she was.

Then she saw the vein pumping at his neck, the throb of his pulse quick and insistent, and knew he wasn't nearly as cool as he appeared.

She couldn't deny the hint of satisfaction the knowledge gave her, even as her unease crept higher at the same time. The tension between them had been growing thicker all day. Clearly, he was just as aware of it as she was.

And now here they were, alone in this room that had been planned with romance in mind, with nowhere to turn.

Clearing his throat gently, he moved toward a small table in the corner. "Well, let's get to work."

Yes, that was exactly what they needed to do, she thought. She watched him go to the small table, realizing there really wasn't enough room for both of them to work at it. A quick scan of the room revealed there was only one other option available to her.

It looked like she would be taking the bed after all.

Alone.

"I'M NOT FINDING MUCH on Julia Bridges," Audrey said a half hour later. Sitting cross-legged on the bed, she looked up from the laptop in front of her and set down the pen she'd been using to take notes on a pad. "It really doesn't look like there's much out there on her."

His expression tense with concentration, Jason didn't

look up from the other laptop they'd bought on their way into Virginia. "That's what I've found, too. Enough to confirm most of what Clint Raymer told us, but not much more than that."

"So now we know that Julia Bridges did grow up as Julie Ann Foster here in Barrett's Mill. She and Rich have been married thirty-three years, thirty-four this July. They were married the summer before he started at the University of Virginia, which must have been right after he returned from Europe. She's a housewife, having dedicated herself to raising their three kids and supporting his career. Ever since he became a senator, she's been active in charitable organizations, but that's about it. I don't show that she's ever even done an interview. It's like you said, she keeps a low profile."

"Normally, I would say that makes her the best kind of political spouse. Chances are, she won't be causing trouble or stirring any controversy for her husband."

"Unless she was the cause of trouble before they were even married," Audrey noted.

"If that's the case, then Dick couldn't have been too happy about the idea of Rich marrying her, whether or not she was from a lower social level like Clint implied."

"I can't imagine Dick intended for his only son to be married at nineteen, not with all the plans he had for him. I'm betting they ran off and eloped without his permission."

"That shouldn't be too hard to confirm. A little digging is all it should take to find out where the marriage took place." He leaned back in his chair. "All right, Marybeth confirmed that Julie Ann dated Tim, so

Clint's story seems to be adding up. Which brings us back to Tim's death."

Audrey nodded. "If Rich was involved somehow, and that was the story Hal uncovered, there must be some way to prove it. Hal wouldn't have relied on Clint Raymer's story alone for the book. If he thought what we're thinking, he would have tried to investigate the crash that killed Tim Raymer, see if there was anything that looked suspicious."

"We can go to the police in the morning, see if there's any way we can see the report on the crash. After all these years, it would be a long shot, assuming a report even existed in the first place. If there was a cover-up, I doubt they would have gone to much trouble to document anything."

"Then we could always track down anyone who was with the police department at that time who's still around, see if they can remember the crash and can tell us anything. And there's always the reporter who covered it for the paper, if he's still around, too."

There was a beat of silence before he admitted, "Exactly what I was about to say."

Grinning, she shot him a pointed look. "I told you, I'm not new at this."

For the slightest of moments, the corners of his mouth began to inch upward. Even that was enough to make her heartbeat pick up slightly.

Then, as though he'd realized what he was about to do, his lips flattened into a thin, unyielding line, just before he turned back to his laptop. "Sounds like we have a plan then."

Audrey surveyed him for a long moment, nearly

shaking her head. Was it just her he didn't want to respond to, or was he so lost in misery that he would deny
himself even a fleeting bit of happiness?

Pretty sure she wouldn't like either answer, she turned
her attention back to the screen in front of her.

Rich and Julia Bridges smiled up at her from one
of the many pictures she'd found of them. They were
always smiling, whether in posed shots or images captured at events. They certainly seemed happy. Whatever
had happened to Tim Raymer, they'd built a fine life for
themselves.

As she had so many times since this had all started,
Audrey studied Richard Bridges's smiling face, trying
to find any trace of the murderer she knew he was.
There wasn't one. She simply saw the same man she
always had, the very image of respectability. Even his
looks were nonthreatening, the kind of bland handsome-
ness that was somehow solid and reassuring. His jaw
was square, his hair thick. Laugh lines were worn into
his skin around the corners of his eyes, giving him the
look of someone who smiled a lot. The eyes themselves
weren't particularly striking, just a comfortable dark
brown. They seemed to shine with warmth and good
humor. It was hard to imagine this man was a murderer,
even though she knew it was true.

Which brought her back to Tim Raymer. She didn't
even know what he looked like, Audrey thought with a
pang. There hadn't been any pictures of him with the
story in the local paper, and nothing had come up online,
probably not surprising for someone who'd been dead
for thirty-five years. She supposed if she really wanted
to know, the local high school probably kept copies of

old yearbooks, or she could even ask Marybeth, for that matter. She hadn't thought to ask Clint, though she doubted he would have held on to any pictures anyway, if he'd ever had any at all.

Just the thought of the man and that dingy house made her feel another twinge of sadness. "Poor Tim," she murmured. "Growing up in that house with that man."

"I can't imagine he was any more pleasant to be around thirty-five years ago," Jason agreed.

"I can understand why Tim was so eager to get away, to make a better life for himself than the one he'd lived until then." She shook her head, exhaling softly. "It's not easy being stuck with a relative who doesn't want you just because there's no one else."

Jason didn't say anything for a moment, then, "Are we talking about Tim now, or about you?"

She blinked at him, only belatedly realizing what she'd said and how it must have come out, the words all too personal. Sending him a sheepish look, she smiled thinly. "I guess it's no secret I know what that's like, huh? Tim wasn't the only one with an uncle who didn't care about him."

He simply looked at her. "Hal cared about you."

Audrey barked out a laugh. "I know he was your friend, but please don't feel the need to defend him. I know he was stuck with me, and he couldn't have cared less about me. It's okay. I came to terms with it a long time ago."

"I'm telling you the truth."

She snorted. "Right. That's why he sent me away to school almost as soon as my parents' funeral was over. That's why he never came to visit me there, why he always sent me to camp in the summer instead of letting me come home with him, why he spent as little time as possible with me on holidays. He missed my high school graduation. I learned my lesson and didn't bother inviting him to my college one, and he never even asked. Hell, I became a journalist and he didn't even notice."

A touch of unexpected sympathy entered his eyes. "That's why you quit being a reporter," he said softly.

It was embarrassing, but she supposed there was no point denying it. "Yeah, well, I finally figured out the real reason I'd pursued it as a career, and I realized there was no use trying to impress someone who simply didn't care." Unable to sit still any longer, she stood up and moved toward the bathroom, having had enough of this conversation. "So forget it. You're wasting your breath, Stone. Not to mention your time and mine."

She was almost to the door when he spoke again.

"At your boarding school graduation you gave a speech. You spoke about how you came to the school shortly after your parents died. You'd lost everything— your family, your home. But most of all, you'd lost your dreams. You were afraid to want anything, dream of anything, because you didn't want to lose everything again. Over the years, you learned a lot at the school, but most of all you learned how to dream again. The teachers who taught you and the friendships you made showed that scared girl how to dream big, that there was too much world out there and too many possibilities to be afraid. You had grown and been changed by what you experienced over those years, and you stood there that day, with everything you'd learned and most of all your dreams, ready to move on and begin making every one of those dreams come true."

She'd stopped halfway through his recitation, her hand on the doorknob, shock holding her in place. Now she clung to the knob for strength, her heart pounding so hard her whole body seemed to be shaking.

Eyes wide, she slowly turned back to face him. He was watching her, no expression on his face.

"How did you know that?" she whispered, barely managing to get the words out.

"Hal told me."

"How could Hal know that?"

"He heard it. He was there."

"No, he wasn't. Believe me, I remember quite clearly that Hal didn't make it to my graduation. I had a seat reserved for him, a seat that remained empty through the ceremony because he never showed. I got a call from him that night apologizing for not making it, saying he got caught up doing something. He didn't even say what, and I didn't ask. The only thing that mattered was that he had better things to do than be there for me."

"He was there," Jason repeated simply. "When he arrived, he saw you getting ready with your classmates, and he was struck dumb by the sight of you. I guess he hadn't seen you in a while. You had your hair down, so it hung to your shoulders, and you were wearing a necklace that belonged to your mother. You looked exactly like her. He was surprised, shocked really. It brought back a lot of memories of your mother, how much he missed her, how it felt losing her. He told me he got a little emotional, but I have a feeling it was more than that, because he stepped out to regain control of himself. By the time he had, the ceremony was beginning. He didn't want to make a scene getting to his seat. Plus, he knew if he sat in the seat you'd saved for him, you would see him, and he didn't want you to see how affected he was. So he stood in the back, and he heard every word. He was moved by what you said, but he also realized how much he'd let you down. Because he hadn't played a part in helping you learn how to dream again. He'd abandoned you there, and in life, because he'd been too afraid himself to get close to you. And when the ceremony was over, he didn't know how to explain why he hadn't been there, sitting in the front row, so he left."

She didn't want to believe it. It wasn't possible; it couldn't be. She tried to think of another explanation. Maybe Hal had gotten a tape of it somehow, though she didn't know why he would have bothered. Maybe someone had told him about it. But that didn't explain why he would have told Jason about it, why he would have made up this story in which he didn't come off well.

No, the most reasonable explanation, unbelievable as it was, was that he really had been there, had really admitted his regrets to Jason.

She knew how close Hal and her mother had been. She remembered his visits when she was a child, how happy her mom had always been to see him, the huge smile on his face whenever he saw her. They'd only been a year apart. It was one reason Audrey had been so confused when he'd rejected her. She'd thought she must have done something wrong. She'd thought he hated her.

"Why didn't he ever say anything?" she asked weakly.

Jason shrugged halfheartedly. "Hal wasn't all that comfortable with emotion. You know how he was."

"No, evidently I didn't. He talked to you about me?"

"Yeah. He used to talk about you a lot before I got married, and then started mentioning you again over the past couple years. The last few conversations we had, he talked more about you than Bridges or the book. He was proud of you. You were at the top of your class all through school. You were doing well as a reporter, making a name for yourself. Then you started your own business from the ground up, and you were successful. You were smart, tough." He paused before continuing awkwardly. "He said you were beautiful. Like I said, you looked exactly like your mother to him."

Audrey frowned. "I don't understand. He talked to you about me before you got married and then in the past couple years..." *In other words, when he was single,* she thought, understanding dawning.

He grimaced and looked away, rubbing the back of his neck with a touch of embarrassment. "It almost seemed like he was trying to set us up."

With a start, she recalled all the things Hal had told her about Jason over the years. There'd been a large gap in those years, now that she thought about it. She'd always thought Hal had simply been raving about his protégé, a man he'd clearly thought a great deal of. Was it possible Hal had actually been trying to build Jason up to her to try to get her interested?

Hal had wanted her to meet Jason, she suddenly remembered. He'd actually spoken about it years ago. She hadn't understood what he was doing, had taken the comment the wrong way. It was shortly after she'd started her career as a reporter, a job she'd taken in a pathetic attempt to win his approval, his attention. And all he'd been able to talk about was Jason, this brilliant young reporter, how she had to meet him. It had felt like an insult, and she resented hearing about the golden boy reporter Hal couldn't stop talking about when he barely seemed to notice her.

She never told Hal she hadn't wanted to meet Jason. He'd simply stopped bringing him up during their occasional conversations. Jason must have met his wife. The only time Hal had mentioned him after that was to say he'd gotten married—until the past couple years, when he'd started bringing him up again.

Dumbfounded, embarrassed, she almost laughed. It seemed so obvious now.

She studied Jason. He was still looking away, the sight of his profile enough to cause a flutter in her belly.

Hal had had good taste, she had to give him that.

That may have explained why Hal had talked about Jason so much with her, and apparently about her so much with him. But it didn't explain everything.

"How did you remember that?" she asked quietly. "What Hal told you about my speech."

He shrugged. "I don't know. Something about the way he described it, the way he talked about you, stuck with me." He finally looked at her again. "Look, losing your mother was hard for him. I'm sure you know how close they were. She was all he had after their folks died. And when she was gone, I think he was afraid to get too close and let himself care about you, in case he lost you, too."

Of course, he would understand that. For a moment, she almost wondered if he was speaking just as much about himself, as she inadvertently had when thinking about Tim Raymer.

As though thinking the same thing she was, Jason cleared his throat. "I'm not saying he was perfect. I'm not saying he did right by you. He knew he didn't. But by the time he realized it, I'm not sure he knew how to make it right. But he did love you. You can believe that."

For the first time in twenty years she did believe it.

Hal had loved her. And now he was gone.

She felt the tears in her eyes moments before they fell and quickly turned before Jason could see them. She had no doubt he knew they were there all the same.

She was still standing at the bathroom door, the knob in her hand. She wanted nothing more than to stumble into the room and absorb everything he'd told her, all the emotions pouring through her, in private.

She couldn't. Not yet. He'd given her a gift, something that meant more to her than he could ever know. She couldn't just walk away without acknowledging that.

She swallowed hard, trying to force down the hard lump that had formed in her throat. Finally, when she thought she could speak clearly, she did.

"Thank you."

"Sure," he said, his voice rough, the tone dismissive, as though what she was thanking him for was nothing. Another man who didn't like talking about emotional things, she registered.

Yet he had, for her.

She didn't want to examine the reasons for his kindness, didn't want to feel this gratitude toward him that only complicated the other emotions he stirred inside her.

Overwhelmed by everything she was feeling, everything he'd just revealed to her about Hal and himself, all she could do was finally step into the bathroom and gently close the door behind her.

CLINT RAYMER SLID onto a stool at the bar and looked around for the bartender. Mickey was at the other end of the bar. Impatient, he rapped his fists on the counter and waited.

He didn't normally make it out to The Rail Spike anymore. It was easier to stay home in his own chair, where he could drink as much as he liked without anybody thinking they knew when he'd had enough and threatening to cut him off. Not to mention the hassle of trying to get home. He didn't kid himself that anyone around here cared much for him, but they sure went out of their way to keep him from driving, like they wouldn't be thrilled if he drove off the road and killed himself one day. Most of the time, coming here was more trouble than it was worth.

But tonight he felt like doing something special. He'd been in a good mood ever since those reporters had left his house.

Now more people knew about Bridges. Soon everybody in the world would.

Clint almost laughed. Richard Bridges. Just another rich bastard who thought he could do whatever he wanted.

About time the world found out he wasn't the damn saint they thought he was.

Mickey finally made his way toward Clint, taking his sweet time of it. "Clint," he said with a nod of acknowledgment. "What can I get you?"

Clint grinned. "Give me something special. I'm celebrating."

"Celebrating, huh?"

"That's right. I was talking to some people today. They're going to get the truth out about Bridges and that little bitch he married. Everybody's going to know the kind of people they really are."

Mickey didn't seem all that impressed. He just gave him a look before moving away, like he didn't believe him.

He would. He'd find out soon enough, just like Bridges.

"Sounds interesting."

Clint glanced over at the man beside him who'd spoken. Clint hadn't noticed him there, or maybe he'd just sat down. He was a big man, muscular with a buzz cut, like he was in the military or something. Clint knew he'd never seen him before. Just another one of the out-of-towners who'd flooded Barrett's Mill.

Clint nodded in acknowledgment. "Oh, believe me, it is."

"I'd love to hear more about it."

Clint squinted at the stranger. "You a reporter, too?"

The man shook his head, the faint traces of a smile on his lips. "Nope. Just someone who likes hearing a good story, and it sounds like you've really got one to tell."

"You've got that right. Bridges probably thought no one'd ever bring it up again or take a good long look at what he really did. He'll never see it coming. That'll make it even better, you know?"

The stranger smiled. "I couldn't agree more."

Chapter Eight

Marybeth Kent pulled a fresh batch of breakfast muffins from the oven, inhaling deeply to draw in the scent of them. The rich aroma failed to have the effect she'd hoped for, doing nothing to ease the tension knotting her stomach. Staring down at the rows of perfectly formed muffin tops, she sighed.

Normally, this was her favorite time of day. Normally, the smells of her kitchen soothed her. The house was quiet, her guests snug in the beds she'd made for them. She loved that feeling, knowing that her house was full of people for whom she'd made a home away from their own homes. It was what she'd always dreamed of, a real home, the kind she hadn't had growing up, and she loved giving that feeling to others.

Except most of the people in her house this morning weren't her normal guests. They were reporters in town because of Richard Bridges.

Richard Bridges, damn him to hell.

She nearly slammed the tray of muffins down on the counter, barely managing to restrain herself at the last moment.

Reining in the response took some effort, and her

hands were shaking as she carefully set down the tray. She took another deep breath, this time to calm herself. When she'd finally stopped shaking, she forced her clenched fingers to ease, then yanked off the oven mitt and began plucking muffins from the tray.

This whole ordeal couldn't be over soon enough. She knew she should be glad for the business. Lord knew, every other business owner in town was thrilled at the revenue generated by all the visitors brought to town by the Bridges hoopla. But none of them had as much reason to hate that name. None of them had a house full of reporters asking too many questions. She was used to putting on a courteous face for even the most challenging guests, but the past week or so had been particularly trying. So many people wanting to know if she knew Richard Bridges, what she thought of him, would she be voting for him.

She almost snorted. Like hell she would.

Because, unlike the whole world—including her own son, she thought with a twinge of pain—she wasn't fooled by Richard Bridges. She knew exactly the kind of man he was.

She'd learned the hard way.

She'd done her best to be polite and decline the reporters' questions gracefully, all while wanting to tell them exactly what she thought of them and their infernal questions—and Richard Bridges. Because he wasn't the only one who'd be hurt by the truth if it came out.

Fear stabbed at her at the thought, and she leaned against the counter to steady herself.

No. No one could ever find out.

Yet the longer the reporters remained in town, the

longer they spent asking questions, looking around, and lurking—always lurking—the more she feared someone would.

Her only guests who weren't reporters were the nice young couple sleeping in Will's room. At first she hadn't been sure whether to believe their story about being honeymooners. They might have been reporters, too, lying with a sympathetic story, in order to get her to rent them a room. But something about them had made her believe them, the way they glanced at each other, that indefinable energy that crackled between them.

She smiled. Yes, there was definitely something romantic between the two of them. She hoped they'd made good use of the room. Normally, she wouldn't feel right about renting Will's room. It wasn't the coziest of spaces, but she figured honeymooners would be more interested in each other than their surroundings anyway. And with them around, at least she had someone under her roof who wasn't obsessed with Richard Bridges.

But this fuss would all be over eventually. She clung to the thought like a lifeline.

In the meantime, all she could do was keep smiling, keep her thoughts to herself, and keep counting the hours until all the reporters, all the other visitors, and most of all, that bastard Richard Bridges, were finally gone and her world was safe once more.

JASON AND AUDREY left the inn a little after eight o'clock. They'd both been up early. After spending more than twelve hours sequestered in that windowless room with her, Jason was more than ready to get out of there. Audrey didn't say anything about it, but he suspected she felt the same way. They managed to slip out of the inn without Marybeth noticing, wanting to avoid having breakfast in the dining room with the other guests in case there was anyone who might recognize him. Not to mention he wasn't up for playing the newlywed this morning.

He kept his eyes on the road, doing his best not to look at her, much as he had ever since their conversation yesterday. Neither of them had mentioned it. When Audrey had reemerged from the bathroom, he'd been back at work, trying to make himself look as busy as possible, leery of what she might say. It turned out he'd worried for nothing. She'd simply returned to her laptop without a word. Eventually, they'd begun speaking about the investigation, but nothing personal had come up again.

It didn't matter. Neither of them had to say anything for it to be obvious something had changed between them, a lowering of the barriers he needed to remain as strong as possible. The knowledge hung there in the air between them. It was impossible for such an intimate conversation not to have an effect on their relationship, the fact that he knew things about her, had been the one to make things personal by sharing them with her, had seen her at her most vulnerable.

He didn't regret telling her. She'd needed to know. The happiness, the gratitude in her eyes when he'd told her that Hal had loved her, had damn near melted every last bit of resistance he felt toward her. In that moment, he hated Hal for not being there for her, and felt a ridiculous amount of pleasure that he'd been the one to cause that look in her eyes.

He'd almost wanted to tell her other things. That she was everything Hal had said she was: strong and smart and beautiful. He'd never really believed Hal when he talked about her all those years ago, or even more recently. She was his niece; of course he was going to exaggerate to make her sound better than she was. He'd had no interest in meeting her, this niece Hal didn't even have a picture of, even before he met Lisa, and especially after what had happened.

But it turned out Hal hadn't exaggerated. Audrey was exactly what he'd said. If anything, he hadn't done her justice. She was even stronger than Hal had said, or maybe even known. Even smarter.

And so beautiful she stirred things in a man who had no business feeling such things, and who damn well didn't want to.

He swallowed hard. No, thankfully he hadn't told her any of that. And he certainly wasn't going to.

He reined in his thoughts of the woman beside him and focused instead on the case as they approached the Barrett's Mill police station. The square one-story building was located on Main Street not far from the library. Jason had to circle the block to find a parking space, finally locating one down the street, and they made their way back to the structure.

Stepping inside, they moved toward the front desk, removing their sunglasses. A uniformed officer looked up as they approached. "Can I help you folks?"

"I hope so," Jason said, working up a smile. "We're doing research on a car accident that happened roughly thirty-five years ago. We were wondering if there's anyone we could speak to about it, or if we could view the police report, if possible."

The officer blinked at him. "That's funny. Somebody was in here a year or so ago asking about an old car crash. About thirty-four, thirty-five years ago, I reckon."

"You wouldn't happen to remember his name, would you?" Audrey asked.

"No, I'm afraid not. It was so long ago."

"Could it have been Hal Talmadge?"

The officer screwed his face up in thought. After a moment he nodded slowly. "Could have been. Sounds about right."

"Did he get to talk to anyone about the crash?" Jason asked.

"I'm afraid not. Like I told him, we're a small department, and nobody who's with the department these days was around back then."

"Did you let him see the report on the crash?"

"No, I told him we wouldn't have it anymore. We don't have any files older than fifteen years or so. Water main broke and flooded the archive room a while back. Anything that old was lost."

"Do you know if anyone who was with the department back then still lives in the area?"

"No, I don't think so."

"What about a coroner or medical examiner?" Audrey asked. "Someone died in the crash, so the ME probably would have examined the body."

A stricken look crossed the officer's face, the expression instantly filling Jason with dread. "Strange that you should ask. Our ME is Doc Foley, or was until last night.

He would have been the ME around thirty-five years ago. But sad to say, there was a fire at old Doc Foley's place last night. The whole place went up. They weren't able to get to him in time."

Jason met Audrey's eyes, reading the same thing there that he was thinking.

Another mysterious fire, another dead person who may have known something.

This wasn't a coincidence. The doctor must have known something after all. Unfortunately, the assassin had gotten to him before they could.

Jason tamped down the anger and frustration that rose in his gut. Damn it. They hadn't just lost another way to the truth. Another life had been lost, all so Richard Bridges could keep his damn secrets.

The bastard had to be stopped.

"Thank you for your help," Jason said, before the officer could start to wonder about the timing of them looking for information the ME could provide the very day after the man died. He wouldn't mind the police figuring out the ME's death wasn't an accident, but he and Audrey couldn't get involved. This was Bridges's town, and Jason wasn't about to trust the local cops with the truth. "I really appreciate it."

He and Audrey quickly made their way out of the station, Jason bracing himself for the officer to call after them.

He didn't. Thirty seconds later they were back on the street.

"Our assassin is tying up loose ends," he murmured under his breath.

"We have to stop him," Audrey said, echoing his

earlier thoughts so completely he couldn't help but glance at her. "Bridges can't get away with all of this."

"We will," he promised her, just as he had himself. He didn't know how they would, but they were going to. "The newspaper office isn't far from here. We can swing by there first, see if the reporter who covered the story still lives in the area—"

"Or if he died recently, too," Audrey murmured.

He couldn't blame her for her dispirited tone. It felt like they were a step behind. It was exactly what they'd considered yesterday. Bridges's man had the book. He knew exactly where to go, exactly whom to stop. They only had to hope there was anyone left, and that there was any chance they could get to that person first.

The newspaper office was a short distance away from the police station. It didn't take them long to get an answer. The current editor informed them the reporter who wrote the story had died twenty years earlier. Furthermore, no one who'd been with the paper thirty-five years ago was still around, either alive or in the area.

Another dead end.

"We should make sure Clint is okay," Audrey suggested, her tone troubled as they moved down the sidewalk. "Just in case."

"Good idea." Not to mention Clint happened to be the best source they had at the moment. Yesterday he'd claimed not to remember the names of anyone else who'd worked at the Bridgeses' farm that summer, but maybe it was early enough that they'd catch him when he was more lucid and capable of remembering.

"Jason Stone?"

Recognizing the voice immediately, Jason nearly

closed his eyes and swore. He did his best not to show any physical reaction, never missing a step or slowing for an instant, even as he admitted it didn't matter. The moment he'd been hoping to avoid as long as possible had arrived.

He'd run into someone he knew, someone who'd clearly recognized him.

Seconds later, a face suddenly appeared in front of him and a hand clapped his shoulder with irritating familiarity. That was Ted Hagan, all affable smiles and big gestures masking a ruthless nature.

He peered into Jason's face with almost ghoulish fascination. "Stone? It is you! I can't believe it."

"Hagan," Jason acknowledged with a tight nod.

"What are you doing here?" Hagan gave his head a vigorous shake. "Like I have to ask. Just couldn't stay away, could you?" The comment was accompanied by another hearty, fake-friendly clap on the shoulder.

"Something like that," Jason said. There was no use denying it. He knew the man wouldn't believe him anyway.

"So how are you doing?" Hagan asked, his face creasing with faked sympathy. As if he cared.

"I'm fine. Thanks for asking."

"Hey, do you want to grab coffee? I'd love to catch up."

Jason was sure he would. "Sorry. I don't think I have time."

"Oh, anything I should know about?"

"No, nothing like that. Nice seeing you." Without another word, he hustled Audrey past the man before Hagan could angle for an introduction.

"Who was that?" Audrey murmured under her breath.

"A columnist for the *Post*," he said shortly. "We're running out of time. Hagan is a gossip. It won't take him long to spread the word around here, and soon every reporter in town will know I'm here. From there, it's only a matter of time before it gets to Bridges's camp, and Bridges himself." It was one thing for their pursuer to suspect they were here. It was another to have him know it for sure. He'd ramp up the search for them. How long could it take before he identified them as the newlywed couple who'd so recently arrived in town?

Jason barely managed to keep from swearing as he and Audrey hurried back to the car. This was bad.

He didn't even want to think about how it could get any worse.

SHAW WAS DRIVING SLOWLY down Main Street, drinking a cup of coffee and carefully examining the face of everyone in sight, when he saw them.

He almost didn't recognize them. They'd dyed their hair, they were wearing sunglasses. But there was something about the woman in particular that grabbed him. She couldn't change the shape of her face, her body, or the way she walked—all of which were distinctly familiar.

And then he saw the man with her, erasing what little doubt remained in his mind.

It was them.

Triumph surged in his veins and he almost smiled. They weren't getting away again.

Shoving the coffee into the cup holder, he stepped

on the accelerator and quickly made a right turn at the next corner. He'd scoped out the town well enough the day before to know the layout of its streets. He quickly went around the block, arriving back on Main Street.

They were climbing into a car parked a short distance ahead, not far from where he'd first spotted them. He pulled over to the curb and waited for them to pull into the street. As soon as they were driving away, he moved into position a short distance behind and started to follow.

After a rough start, this was all working out well.

And now it was time to finish it.

He listened to the sound of the gasoline sloshing around in the tanks he'd stashed in the backseat, the noise reminding him of the plan. And this time he did grin.

Sometimes the best ideas came from books.

"AT LEAST NOW WE KNOW there must have been more to Tim Raymer's death than a simple car accident," Audrey said, thinking out loud as they made their way to Clint's house. "Something that must have been apparent in the autopsy, and which the medical examiner knew about. It's the only reason they would have killed him."

"The ME must have told Hal." Jason picked up her train of thought. "It's the only logical reason to go after him now. Hal must have written about it in the book, and that's how they knew the ME had to be silenced."

"So, in all likelihood Tim Raymer's death was the secret Hal had uncovered for the book. Hal must have had enough to prove Rich Bridges was involved some-how, but how are *we* going to? We can't prove that the

ME knew anything, and it doesn't sound like there's anyone else around who might have known what he did."

Jason remained silent for a long moment before finally conceding, "I don't know."

She could tell it had been hard for him to admit that. It wasn't any easier to hear. He'd known what they should do every step of the way until now. To have him finally be at a loss indicated just how serious things were.

The plan had been to release the story so the truth Hal had died to reveal came out. But if they couldn't do that, there seemed to be no way of stopping Bridges.

She fell as silent as he had, desperately trying to come up with a new plan, a new direction, anything at all. She still didn't have one by the time Jason turned onto the road leading to Clint Raymer's house.

As she had the day before, Audrey stared at the passing trees outside her window, this time hardly seeing them. She'd been fighting a sense of hopelessness that had started to build the moment the police officer had told them about the ME's death. Foley, the officer had said his name was. Doc Foley. She didn't even know his first name, but he was another victim in this, someone else who died to keep Richard Bridges's secrets.

So many deaths. And as their pathways of getting to the truth were systematically closed off, Audrey couldn't shake the feeling that there would be more.

She was so lost in her thoughts she almost missed the flash of color that shouldn't have been there. As it was, she didn't register what she'd seen until a few seconds later.

She leaned forward in her seat, looking back. "Did you see that?"

"What?" Jason asked.

"I think I saw something through the trees. Go back."

He didn't ask any other questions, simply stopping the car and shifting into Reverse. They both turned around as the vehicle rolled backward, Audrey keeping a close eye out for what she'd seen.

There it was. A gap in the trees where she was sure there hadn't been one yesterday.

"Stop," she said. He immediately brought the car to a halt. Audrey quickly unbuckled her seat belt and scrambled out of the vehicle. Even before she reached the edge of the road, she saw what had caught her attention. An unmistakable patch of blue amidst all the greenery. Stopping at the steep edge of the road, she stared down at the blue object jutting out of the ditch.

It was the truck they'd seen parked in front of Clint Raymer's house yesterday, presumably his own. What she'd seen was part of the back panel, which was elevated enough to be visible from the road.

She felt Jason come up beside her. "Do you think there's any chance Clint's not in there?" Audrey whispered.

"I'll climb down and check. If he is, he could still be alive."

He won't be, she thought, despair washing over her. Still, she waited as he quickly climbed down to the truck, glancing over her shoulder at the road to see if anyone approached. No one did.

Jason finally reappeared. As soon as she spotted him,

Audrey reached for his arm and helped him back onto the surface. "Well?" she asked.

He shook his head tersely, his expression tight. "He's dead. Looks like several hours at least. The body and the engine were cold."

"We should have warned him more," Audrey murmured.

"We tried," he said gently, thankfully not trying to convince her this had simply been an accident.

"Should we call someone? The police?"

He was quiet for a long moment. "I'm not sure we can," he said finally. "I don't think we should get too involved with the police. If they look into our story at all, they'll probably figure out it's not true. Besides, I don't know how close they are to Bridges, and I don't think we can risk it. Even an anonymous call could be traced in a town this small."

With one last glance in the direction of the truck, Audrey nodded her agreement. She knew he was right. Even though Clint Raymer hadn't been a good man, or much of an uncle to his nephew, she wasn't happy the man was dead. But if not reporting his death meant they were safer for a little longer, she could live with that.

"When they find him, they'll just think it was an accident, won't they?"

Jason grimaced. "He smelled pretty heavily of alcohol. Whether he'd been drinking or splashed with liquor to make it seem that way, I'm sure they'll conclude he was driving drunk, especially given his reputation around here."

Under different circumstances, she would probably come to the same conclusion. But given everything else that had happened recently, there wasn't a doubt in her mind this had been murder.

Another murder that would be declared an accident, unless the truth about Bridges was exposed.

If only she had any idea how to do it.

Exhaling sharply, she started to shake her head, frustration and anger churning in her belly. It wasn't right. There had to be a way—

"Hey."

Jason suddenly moved closer, placing his hands on her upper arms. She blinked up to find him peering down at her, his gaze steady and reassuring.

"It's going to be okay," he said gently.

A bleak smile touched her lips. "Is it?"

He answered firmly, without hesitation. "Yes."

"How?" she asked simply, wanting nothing more than to believe him, to hear he had an answer to this mess.

His expression lost none of its certainty, but all he said was, "I don't know yet. But it will. We'll figure it out."

She forced a nod, wishing she felt anywhere near the confidence she heard in his voice.

Then it finally struck her how close he was standing, that he was touching her. In an instant, something changed. The frustration and hopelessness faded as warmth suddenly poured into her system, a response to his nearness, to his steady gaze, to the feeling of those gloved hands on her arms.

She knew immediately he'd done it without thinking, saw him realize what he'd done just as she had, his eyes widening slightly with surprise. His fingers tensed and stilled on her arms, as though he was on the verge of pulling them away. She froze, not wanting to lose the contact, willing him to not let her go.

He didn't. He simply stood there, his hands locked on her arms, his eyes fixed on hers. She watched as they seemed to burn with a fresh heat, the sight of it stoking the same reaction inside her, along with a knowing thrill.

He may not want to live, but there was no doubting that he was still alive, his response to her clear. The emotions played across his face, flickered in his eyes, too strong to be hidden. Just as the firm hold he kept on his emotions had been unable to stop the impulse to move closer and comfort her. The compulsion had been too strong to be denied.

Why? she wondered, even as part of her was afraid to know the answer, even as part of her wanted more. If only she could lean into him and feel his arms around her. If only he would pull her close and truly make her believe that everything was going to be all right.

She stood there, held in his hands, in his gaze, and waited for it. Waited for him to do something, anything that matched the heat in his eyes.

Instead, he finally released her. His hands dropped from her arms and he took a step back, lowering his eyes.

"We should go."

Swallowing a sigh, she nodded again. "Yeah," she said softly. "We should."

They climbed back into the car without another word. Jason managed to turn the vehicle around on the narrow road, and they headed back to the main one.

Audrey stared steadily out her window, once again

watching the trees, her mood even gloomier than before. It didn't matter that she hadn't liked Clint Raymer. It was just as she'd predicted minutes earlier. Another death. How many more would there be?

She sat unmoving, so when they reached the intersection, her head was already turned to the right. Jason slowed to a stop to check before turning onto the road. That was when she saw the car.

It was pulled off on the shoulder a short distance down the road facing them. The sight of it was strange, the car just sitting there on the side of this empty stretch of road outside of town. She tried to remember if it had been there when they'd first come this way and turned onto Clint's road, only to admit she hadn't been paying close enough attention to notice.

Then, as she watched, it began to roll forward, just as Jason pulled onto the road.

Unease sliding through her, she checked the side mirror. Sure enough, the car had fallen into line behind them, gradually gaining speed.

She couldn't see the driver through the windshield. She didn't need to. Somehow she just knew.

"Jason," she said, "we have company."

"I see him," he murmured.

"It's him, isn't it?"

"I would bet on it," Jason said grimly.

She never looked away from the mirror, wondering what the driver was planning. Simply to follow them back to town?

No, the car was picking up speed too quickly, she realized, alarm raising prickles along her skin. It was gaining on them too fast, even as she felt Jason accelerate.

Two seconds later, it shot over into the other lane and began to pull alongside them.

Audrey whipped her head toward the other vehicle. She caught flashes of the driver. It was the man she'd seen outside the diner all right. He was hunched over the wheel, his face grim with determination.

Then he glanced over at them, his eyes narrowed. A split second later he jerked the wheel to the right.

The car swerved into them, ramming their car from the side. Audrey crashed against her door, pain jolting through her shoulder and arm. Their car skidded onto the side of the road, kicking up dirt and rocks. Jason managed to keep the vehicle moving straight as the two cars bounced apart, the other vehicle lurching back into the left lane.

He's trying to force us off the road, she thought numbly, trying to make sense of it. Why would he? It would look too much like Clint's death, wouldn't it? Wouldn't it be too suspicious?

Evidently, he didn't care. A moment later, the car slammed into them again.

The impact was harder, or maybe it seemed that way. She cringed at the pain that screamed through her. They were knocked farther over onto the shoulder, until it seemed like they were teetering on the edge before Jason managed to get them back in the lane.

"What are we going to do?" she asked.

"Just wait," he muttered, never taking his eyes off the road, his face tight with concentration.

She looked past him, to the other driver, his car keeping pace beside them once more.

Their eyes met across the distance.

He grinned at her, the malice in the expression turning her blood cold.

"Hang on!" Jason yelled.

Before she could process the words, he suddenly slammed on the brakes.

She was thrown against her seat belt, her head snapping forward, the impact knocking the air from the lungs. Her head jerked upright just in time to see the other car slide by sideways in front of them.

She watched in amazement as it seemed to float by almost in slow motion, its tires screeching, the driver no doubt trying to gain traction.

He didn't make it. The car shot straight off the road, vanishing over the rim of the shoulder.

Moments later the deafening sounds of a crash met her ears.

She stared in shock, seeing what lay before them, what she hadn't noticed before, what the other man clearly hadn't, finally understanding what had happened.

They'd just reached a curve in the road. Directly in front of them, the road wound left sharply. Jason had braked at exactly the right time, and the other driver had tried to swerve over and hit them at exactly the wrong time. Without their car to stop his momentum, he'd flown right over the curve in the road.

Jason immediately swerved onto the shoulder and stopped the car, jumping out almost before he'd shifted it into Park. Though still in shock, Audrey did the same.

Jason skidded to a stop at the edge of the road, peering down to where the car had landed. It had apparently flipped over a few times, ending up on its roof.

Then a flash of light suddenly erupted inside the

vehicle. She watched in amazement as flames burst to life inside the windows.

The car was on fire.

She half wondered if they should try to save the driver, even as she acknowledged they couldn't. It was too dangerous. The rest of the car could go up at any moment.

The man was going to burn to death in his car.

Just like Tim Raymer, or at least how he'd supposedly died. Somehow, it seemed poetic justice that the man willing to kill to conceal the truth of Tim's death should die in the same way.

Or maybe it wasn't just poetic, but deliberate, she thought, as the smell of gasoline reached her on the breeze.

She frowned. There hadn't been an explosion like the gas tank blowing up. The inside of the car had simply caught fire. It didn't make sense. Why would the inside of the car catch fire so quickly?

Unless he'd had gasoline inside the car. But why—

This was the death he'd planned for them, she realized. Merely forcing them off the road wasn't guaranteed to kill them. No, he would have had to do more than that to make sure they were dead, maybe to make sure their identities weren't discovered for as long as possible. To do that, he would have set them on fire. That was why he'd brought the gasoline.

Instead, that death had turned out to be his.

Poetic indeed, she thought darkly, unable to summon the slightest bit of sympathy.

Then she glanced at Jason, again reminded that

while Tim Raymer may not have died in a burning car, others had.

He stared at the inferno, unblinking, his expression unreadable. She remembered his reaction to the mere description of Tim Raymer's death in the paper. She could only imagine what seeing an actual car in flames must be like for him, the memories it must bring back.

Audrey gently placed her hand on his forearm. A little charge passed through her fingers at the contact. She ignored it. "Are you all right?" she asked again.

He didn't answer immediately, continuing to stare at the flames. Finally, he gave his head a little shake.

"I'm fine." He glanced over at her and frowned, his eyes stroking her face with an intensity that sent another charge through her. "Are *you* all right?"

A smile touched her lips. "Still alive. That's all that matters, right?"

To her surprise he smiled faintly, a ghost of one that was still incredibly potent when seen on his normally stoic face. "That's right," he said softly.

As expected, the smile quickly faded. "We need to get out of here," he murmured. "We can't be found here."

He reached for her arm and she immediately fell into step beside him. "I assume you don't want to report this either."

"No. I'm sure someone will come along soon enough. When Bridges finds out his assassin is dead, he'll move to replace him. No one knowing buys us some time."

Yes, some *time,* she thought as they returned to the car. But not nearly enough. Their pursuer had only been one man, but if Bridges could send one, he could certainly send others.

Meanwhile, she still didn't have any idea whom they could turn to for answers who might be able to help them prove what they believed they knew.

They may have gained a little time, but it seemed they were still flat out of options.

Chapter Nine

Richard Bridges stood at the second-floor window and watched the preparations unfolding on the lawn behind the house. He'd arrived at the farm only an hour ago, and there were numerous things he should be doing. He needed to review the speech he was set to give tomorrow, the biggest speech of his life to date. His staff needed his input on various matters. And of course, Dick wanted to speak with him. That was nothing new—Dick always wanted to speak with him about something—but the man had been even more demanding over the past several months. Rich could only imagine what he'd be like over the next few years, let alone the years to follow, if he won.

But of course, first he had to officially declare his candidacy.

Below, the stage had been built and the podium set in place. He took in the multitude of signs and posters, the banner waiting to be unfurled. The sight did little to reduce the uneasiness that had been nagging at him more and more as this day approached.

Because, instead of the future, he found himself thinking more and more about the past.

Once he took that stage, once he gave that speech, he would be subject to a greater scrutiny than any he'd ever faced. Massive numbers of people would dedicate themselves to going over every bit of his life history, prepared to drag out the slightest bit of dirt and bare it to the harsh light of day.

A terrifying thought for anyone, to have their secrets exposed to the world, but even more so for someone who actually had something to hide.

He'd never thought it possible that anyone would find out. There was simply no way.

But now he wondered more and more if there was any way it *wouldn't* be.

Sighing, he turned away from the window. Over the years, he'd never felt a single regret for anything he'd done. Why should he? All anyone could do in this life was do the best with the circumstances they were given. He'd done exactly what he had to, made the necessary choices, the hard decisions.

But was it all worth it?

Not too long ago he would have answered yes. He wouldn't be here if he hadn't made the choices he had, and this was exactly where he should be. He knew he was the right man to lead this country. He knew how much good he could do. It was for a greater good, not just his own, that he was prepared to fight for the presidency.

So why did he feel this persistent unease growing stronger every day?

Perhaps because now that he was on the verge of attaining so much, it simply reminded him of just how much he had to lose. And if anyone found out the truth, the choice he'd made so long ago, he *would* lose everything, he had no doubt about that. People wouldn't understand. They would judge, as people inevitably did.

Of course, that was only *if* the truth came out.

And so, all he could do was move forward, prepare for the moment he'd been working for his entire adult life, and keep praying that the secrets they'd all worked so hard to bury remained that way.

AUDREY AND JASON were quiet on the drive back to the inn. She knew they were both searching for a solution to their current situation, another way to get to the truth. When neither of them had spoken by the time they arrived, she guessed that meant he hadn't come up with answers any more than she had.

The front desk was empty as they came through the door. Audrey was grateful for that, not really up to pretending to be happy for Marybeth's benefit.

"I'm going to take a shower and change," Jason said. She glanced at him, remembering how he'd climbed into the ditch. His clothes were rumpled and smudged with dirt.

Her stomach suddenly rumbled, the discovery that she could still be hungry at a time like this surprising her. She realized they hadn't eaten anything today. "I think I'll stay up here," she told him. "It's almost lunchtime. I'll see if Marybeth has something to eat."

With a nod, he headed for the back stairs. Trying to fight the discouragement weighing down on her, Audrey moved through the foyer into the dining room.

As she walked through the room toward the kitchen, she noticed some of Will Kent's campaign materials spread out on a sideboard. Curious, she slowed to take a look, picking up one of the full-color flyers.

He really was quite handsome, and very photogenic, she acknowledged, taking in the face smiling up at her. Probably a good thing for a politician. He had solid, all-American good looks, his jaw square and strong, his teeth straight and blindingly white. The photographer had managed to capture his charisma, and the charm in Will's smile came across in the picture as well as it did in real life. On a professional level, she had to admire the photographer's skill.

Audrey started to lower the flyer back to the table, but something made her stop, the image holding her attention. There was something else about him, something about the shape of his face around his eyes…

The eyes themselves were brown. She remembered Marybeth's were blue, so Will must have gotten his eyes from his father.

Brown eyes. Eyes that were warm and reassuring, full of good humor.

Eyes that were a lot like another pair of eyes she'd found herself studying so intently recently…

Audrey stared, dumbstruck, as recognition hit her.

Her first instinct was to wonder if she was imagining things. She had Richard Bridges on the brain. It was completely plausible that she would start seeing him everywhere.

But as she quickly registered the other facial features Will hadn't inherited from his mother, all of them very familiar, certainty took hold within her, until there was no denying it.

Will Kent was Richard Bridges's son.

Most people might not notice, but this was what she did for a living. She looked at faces, examined people's images. She knew how to recognize a familial resemblance. After all the time she'd spent studying Richard Bridges's face over the past few days, she could clearly see its influences in Will Kent's. Will looked like his mother; she'd seen that from the start. But the features that didn't bear Marybeth's influences were uncannily Richard Bridges's.

Will appeared to be in his mid-thirties. Audrey wished she knew exactly when he'd been born. Perhaps roughly nine months after that summer thirty-five years ago? It should be easy enough to find out.

She shook her head in amazement. It seemed so hard to believe. But as she remembered Marybeth's response to Bridges's name and to the mention of Julie Ann Foster, it made too much sense not to be true.

Audrey was still trying to absorb the revelation when Marybeth pushed through the swinging door from the kitchen and stepped into the dining room.

She blinked at Audrey in surprise. The smile that had started to automatically form on her lips faded as she took in Audrey's expression. "Lila, is everything all right?"

At first Audrey could only blink back at her, unsure what she should say, if she could even admit what she'd discovered. But of course, she had to. This was why she and Jason had come to Barrett's Mill, to uncover Rich Bridges's secrets, the things he would do anything to keep hidden. Audrey had to figure out what to do about it. But first she had to know if it was true.

She sent a glance behind her. The last thing she

wanted was to have this conversation overheard. "Is there somewhere we can talk privately?"

Marybeth's frown deepened, and a touch of wariness shone in her eyes. Audrey had a feeling the woman would like to ask what she wanted to talk about. Instead, because of her innkeeper's politeness, or because she recognized something in Audrey's expression, she nodded and said, "All right."

She turned and moved back through the swinging door. Audrey followed close behind.

Marybeth stepped behind the kitchen counter and braced her hands on it, facing Audrey. "What can I do for you?"

Audrey tried to choose her words carefully, knowing just how tough this was going to be. "I need to ask you about your son…and Richard Bridges."

Marybeth's brow furrowed in confusion, but Audrey caught the flash of alarm in the other woman's eyes. "I don't understand."

"Is Richard Bridges Will's father?"

"That's absurd," Marybeth scoffed. Audrey might have imagined it, but the woman's bluster sounded false to her ear.

She made herself go on. "Thirty-five years ago, Richard Bridges spent the summer before he was supposed to go to college here in Barrett's Mill, until he abruptly left for Europe. There were rumors that he was involved with a local girl at the time."

"Julie Ann Foster," Marybeth said, her eyes narrowing, her cheeks going red with a trace of anger Audrey doubted she even knew she'd shown.

"It makes sense," Audrey agreed. "But just because

he was involved with one girl doesn't mean he wasn't involved with another. When was Will born?"

"None of your business."

"Maybe not, but I can find out. I would guess it was about nine months after that summer. Will's about thirty-four, isn't he?"

"That doesn't mean anything."

"Marybeth, I don't think I mentioned it, but I'm a photographer. Family portraits, school photos, that sort of thing. I look at people's faces every day, and what I finally saw when I really looked at Will's was a resemblance to Richard Bridges. I think if anyone puts two pictures of them side-by-side, others will see it, too, and they'll start wondering. Then they'll start looking into Will's family history—your past—to see if there's an explanation. What do you think they'll find?"

"Nothing," Marybeth whispered. "They won't find anything."

"Are you sure about that?" Audrey asked gently, though Marybeth's expression said she was anything but.

Marybeth swallowed hard. "You're not here on your honeymoon, are you?" she asked faintly.

"No," Audrey admitted. "And my name isn't Lila Randall. It's Audrey Ellison. My uncle was a man named Hal Talmadge. I don't know if you've heard of him, but he was here in Barrett's Mill last year."

It took a moment before Marybeth slowly nodded. "I remember. He was talking to people, asking questions."

"Did he talk to you at all?"

"No," Marybeth said, practically a whisper.

So, in all likelihood, Hal hadn't found out about this. It made sense. The assassin hadn't come after Marybeth, so she probably wasn't mentioned in the book.

"He was a journalist working on a book about Richard Bridges, particularly his early years. That's why he was here. He was doing research for the book. From the way he talked about it, he thought he'd found out something about Richard Bridges, a secret or scandal he was going to reveal in the book. He was murdered a few days ago, and someone has been trying to kill me and the man pretending to be my husband ever since. We're pretty sure Richard Bridges is responsible. We think he's trying to silence anyone Hal might have told what he learned."

Audrey watched the woman's reaction. Her eyes widened, but she displayed none of the shock Audrey might have expected. "You don't seem surprised."

Marybeth exhaled sharply, her lips twisting with bitterness. "Nothing Rich Bridges does could surprise me anymore."

"So you do know him," Audrey said carefully. "Or at least you did. I'm guessing thirty-five years ago?"

After a moment, Marybeth nodded slowly. "Yes," she said, barely more than a whisper.

"And the two of you became involved?"

Another nod. "I met him for the first time that summer. He never really was around the local kids much. We knew who he was, but he usually stuck to the farm when he was in town over the summer. I always thought he was just some stuck-up rich kid. But then I met him in town one day. It was the kind of thing you see in movies, when two people meet and just click. I looked at him and it didn't matter who he was or how ridiculous it was, I thought, this is the boy I'm going to marry. I'm sure that sounds like I was trying to hook a rich husband, but it wasn't like that. There was just something about him, and I knew he was the one.

"We got to talking. He wasn't anything like I'd thought he would be. He was…sweet and shy. His mother was dead and he was being raised by his father, like I was, and neither of our fathers had much use for us. After that first meeting, it wasn't long until we were spending every possible moment with each other. Dick wasn't around much that summer, but Rich said if anyone told him about the two of us, he wouldn't like it. So we had to sneak around. I didn't care. I just wanted to be with him."

"Then you found out you were pregnant?"

"I was scared, but I told Rich right away. He seemed so happy. He—" She swallowed hard. "He asked me to marry him right then and there. He said he wanted us to be a family." She winced as though the memory was painful. "Of course I said yes. I hadn't wanted it to happen like that, but it was basically what I'd dreamed of from the moment I met him."

"Then what happened?" Audrey asked.

"Dick Bridges was coming home that night. Rich was going to tell him about me, about the baby, that he was going to marry me. I offered to go with him, to be there while he did it. He said it would be better if he did it by himself, that Dick wasn't going to be happy and he didn't want to subject me to that, but he'd come see me as soon as it was done. I waited all night for him to come. He never did.

"Finally, I went out to the farm. The housekeeper told me Rich had left, gone to Europe. She didn't have any way to reach him and didn't expect him to be back anytime soon. I didn't want to believe it. He wouldn't have just left like that. I kept waiting for him to get in touch with me. He would call, he would write. I *knew* it. But he didn't. In the meantime, all I could think about was how I was going to be a single mother at eighteen, trying to raise a baby on my own, what it would be like for the baby to grow up knowing his father hadn't wanted him.

"I had a friend, Adam Kent. He found me crying one day, and I told him I was pregnant and the baby's father was gone and I didn't know what to do. He didn't ask any questions. He just asked me to marry him. He was barely out of high school himself, but that was the kind of man he was. I didn't think that was fair to him, but he said it would be his honor. I never even knew he thought of me that way before then. I didn't know what else to do. So I said yes. My father wasn't too happy about it, but he was even less happy with the idea of his unmarried eighteen-year-old daughter having a baby. Less than a week later, Adam and I were married."

"And no one ever knew he wasn't Will's father?"

"No."

"Did you ever speak to Rich again?"

"No. He never contacted me again, and I didn't try. I didn't want to see his face again." She exhaled sharply. "And then he went and became a senator and decided he wanted to run for president. Now I can't get away from him."

"And Will still doesn't know the truth?"

"No. As far as he knows, Adam Kent was his father. And he *was,* in every way that matters. He's the one who held Will on the day he was born. He's the one who coached him in Little League and taught him how to ride a bike. He's the one who taught Will how to be the man he is today. He was a better father than Rich Bridges ever could have been, and I won't let that be taken away from Will.

"I'm sorry about what happened to your uncle and what's happening to you now, but I told you this so you'd see that my son and I are victims of the Bridgeses, too. I don't think you can prove that Rich is Will's father, but you can make things messy for Rich. But you'll also make things a lot harder for Will. He's the one who'll be hurt in this, much more than Rich."

Marybeth suddenly reached out and placed her hand over Audrey's. "Please," she whispered. "My son deserves better than to be known as nothing more than Richard Bridges's bastard. He has a future. He's his own man. Please don't take that away from him."

Audrey's heart twisted at the woman's plea. Marybeth was right. She and Will would be hurt if the truth came out, and Audrey didn't want to hurt anybody. But at the same time, her life and Jason's were on the line, and this was something they could use against Bridges to save themselves. And people needed to know what kind of man Bridges was. Part of her wished she could give the woman the assurance she clearly wanted, the rest knew she had to remain silent. Torn, she could only stare into the other woman's eyes and wish she knew what to say.

Someone knocked on the swinging door to the

kitchen, startling them both. They both looked back toward the door just before it was slowly pushed open.

Jason stuck his head through the opening, his gaze centering on Audrey moments before he stepped fully into the room. "There you are. I was wondering where you were."

He must have noticed the undercurrents in the room. His eyes narrowing slightly, he glanced from her to Marybeth and back again. "Is everything okay?"

"Come in," Audrey said. "We have to a lot to talk about."

A HALF HOUR LATER, Jason sat at the kitchen table with Audrey and Marybeth, mulling over everything they'd told him.

He shook his head in amazement. "Bridges really is a piece of work. He plays the good guy so well you'd never think he's capable of something like this."

"He's fooled a lot of people," Marybeth agreed quietly, her own experience weighing heavily in her tone.

Anger jolted through him at what she'd been through, the way Bridges had abandoned her. "People need to know the kind of man he really is."

Then he saw the fear that flashed in Marybeth's eyes and the worry in Audrey's, and his anger quickly gave way to frustration. He knew what Audrey was thinking. She hadn't had to say a word; he'd read it in her face as she and Marybeth had related the story. She didn't want to hurt the Kents. He didn't want to either. The only person he was interested in seeing hurt in all of this was Bridges. He just didn't know if there was a way to do it without inflicting a lot of collateral damage.

His instinct had once been to hold the truth above all else, but no more. No, he couldn't do that to Marybeth or Will, couldn't be responsible for hurting them, turning their private histories into headlines, even to bring down someone who deserved it. He and Audrey couldn't reveal this secret.

But of course, Bridges didn't know that.

As soon as the thought occurred to him, inspiration struck, and he knew exactly what they had to do.

"We need to talk to Bridges."

Both women frowned at him. "What do you mean?" Audrey asked.

"The original plan was to release whatever information we found, whatever secret Hal had uncovered. We can't do that because we can't prove any of it. But he doesn't know that. Our only way out of this is to threaten to release the information if he doesn't leave us alone, and convince him that we'd actually do it. Holding the information over him is our only guarantee he won't come after us anymore."

Audrey's frown merely deepened. "But then people won't find out the truth about him. He'll get away with all of it."

"And you'll be alive."

Her eyes narrowed. "You mean *we'll* be alive."

"The point is, it's a chance for survival, the only one I can think of. Unless you have any better ideas."

She shook her head. "I don't. So what do you want to do, call him?"

"No, this has to be done face-to-face. It's the only way we can show him we mean business and that we we'll be able to see whether or not he's telling the truth if he agrees. We need to get close to him."

She gaped at him. "That's going to be impossible. He has so many people around him at all times, there's no way we'll ever get anywhere near him."

"Maybe we can disguise ourselves."

"Except that you've already been recognized. By now that man Hagan will have gotten the word out that you're in town. All of Bridges's people could have been alerted to keep an eye out for you at all times."

She was right. He tried to come up with another option, another way to get close to Bridges. But the man was surrounded by people at all times. Besides his own private security, he would soon have Secret Service protection, if he didn't already.

When someone finally spoke, it wasn't him or Audrey.

"I know a way," Marybeth said quietly.

They both looked at her. "You do?" Audrey asked, clearly just as surprised as Jason was.

"He's at the house for the campaign event, isn't he?" she said. "There's a tunnel that leads from the edge of the property right into the house. Rich used to use it to get out, or to bring me in without anyone noticing. That's how no one knew about us that summer. There's access to several of the bedrooms on the second floor, including the one that was always Rich's."

"Do you think the tunnel's still there?" Audrey asked.

"I don't see why it wouldn't be. It was built over two hundred years ago, when the house was. It seems that the early Bridgeses weren't any more reputable than the current breed. They had their share of shady dealings, and they needed a secret way to escape from the house, so they built the tunnel."

He and Audrey exchanged a glance. It seemed too good to be true. Should they trust her? Marybeth didn't want the truth of Will's paternity getting out any more than Bridges did. This could be her way of setting them up to be caught, captured, killed.

Then again, she could also be trusting that they wouldn't tell anyone about her son's paternity, wouldn't leave word in case they didn't survive.

Not to mention, they didn't have many other options.

Audrey gave him a small nod, the resolve in her eyes matching his own.

It appeared they didn't have any choice.

Chapter Ten

"I almost can't believe Bridges was willing to wage a presidential campaign with all this dirt out there just waiting to be discovered," Audrey said later that night when they were alone in their room. "Even if the truth of Tim Raymer's death was reasonably hidden, Will Kent is a much more visible person. I can't be the only one who will have noticed the resemblance."

Seated at the small table, Jason had to agree with her. It seemed strange that the Bridgeses had let Marybeth have her baby and raise it alone without guaranteeing she'd never reveal the child's father. Maybe they'd figured that if Marybeth hadn't done so during Bridges's earlier senate runs, she wasn't going to now. Still, it would have made sense for them to get some assurances of that rather than ignore her completely.

At the same time, nothing people did really surprised him anymore. "Some people are arrogant enough to think they can get away with anything. Just look at all the politicians caught having affairs."

"Yes, that's why I said 'almost,'" she said with a wry smile. "I guess there's really no end to what people will fool themselves into thinking they can get away with."

"Well, he's going to learn, like so many others before him, that he can't get away with everything."

"Do you really think this is going to work?"

Jason considered his answer carefully, then finally admitted, "I don't know."

He watched her frown and wished he was the kind of person who could lie to her. He doubted she would believe him—she had to know the risks as well as he did—but being honest seemed cruel at the moment.

Marybeth had given them directions to the tunnel's entrance and they'd driven out to check it out beforehand. It was exactly where she'd said it was, well hidden off the farm property and a half a mile from the house, in a small cluster of woods. It would have been impossible to find without her directions, the trapdoor built into the ground and covered with leaves and undergrowth. From the looks of it, and the ancient padlock attached to it, the door hadn't been opened in years and Stone hadn't spotted any security measures around it. While security would undoubtedly be high around the farm tomorrow, it appeared that this entrance had been overlooked.

They were going in early the next morning. If they were going to see Bridges, they needed to do it at a time when he was likely to be alone. Bursting in during the middle of the night would probably get them shot on sight; going in too late could result in missing him entirely. Their best chance would be to catch him when he was getting ready in the morning, alone and awake enough to be convinced to hear them out rather than calling for help right away.

The thought of everything that could go wrong reminded him of how crazy this plan was, how much of a risk they both were taking when only one of them needed to.

"I still think it would be better if I did this alone," he said.

Audrey sent him a sardonic look. "I know. You already said that. And you might as well forget it. I'm not letting you go in there alone."

"If something happens to me, you'll still be alive and able to figure another way out of this."

"If something happens to you and I don't immediately release any information, he'll know I don't have anything to release, so I won't have any leverage anyway. Besides, one person going in alone is just plain foolish. You need someone to have your back, otherwise it might as well be a suicide mission." Her gaze sharpened. "At least one of us cares whether you live or die. I'm going."

He opened his mouth to argue further, only to recognize there wasn't much point. He recognized that stubborn gleam in her eye well enough by now. Saying anything else would just be wasted breath.

He wanted to be irritated with her for being willing to risk her life for his, but all he felt was a grudging respect he'd never admit. "Fine," he muttered.

"Good." Audrey relaxed slightly. She was silent for a few moments before shaking her head. "Even if it does work, it seems wrong that the story Hal died to tell won't come out. The truth will remain buried. Doesn't it bother you that there won't be any justice for Hal, or the medical examiner, or even Clint Raymer, not to mention Tim?"

"All I care about is you not being killed."

"What about the truth?"

"Trust me, the truth doesn't count for much if people are hurt trying to get it. Was this story really worth Hal dying over, or Clint or the ME?"

"I think Hal would have said so. Bridges is probably going to be the next president. Don't people deserve to know what kind of man he really is?"

"I've already made the mistake of worrying about other people instead of the ones that really mattered. I won't do it again."

Only when the words were out did he consider how they might have come across—like she mattered to him.

Which she did, he immediately recognized, his chest tightening at the thought. He didn't want it to be the case, but the feeling was undeniable, even if he'd only admit it to himself. This woman had come to mean something to him in the past several days, enough so that the idea of anything happening to her scared the hell out of him.

If she'd noticed the implication, she didn't show it. She simply looked at him, so much sympathy in her eyes he had to glance away. "What happened to your family wasn't your fault."

"Yes, it was," he said roughly. "Make no mistake, it was."

"You couldn't have known there was a bomb in the car."

"But I did know the kind of people I was dealing with. I could have anticipated how they may have re-acted to my investigation. I could have thought about my family—but I didn't. All I cared about was the story. And they were the ones who paid for it."

"Is that why you don't want to live? The guilt?"

"I never said I don't want to live," he said weakly.

"You never said you do either."

No, he hadn't. He remembered that all too well. He hadn't been able to say it, just like he couldn't say it now.

He wished he could, if only to get her to stop talking, even though he doubted she would believe him. But no matter how much he tried to summon them, the words wouldn't come.

When he didn't say anything, she finally asked, "Don't you think they would have wanted you to live?"

Jason exhaled sharply. "They're not around to offer their opinions, now are they? That's the point."

"They loved you, didn't they? Your wife? Your little girls? Just as much as you loved them."

No, he almost said. They couldn't have. No one could love anyone as much as he'd loved them, not even them. It simply wasn't possible.

Instead he said nothing, *couldn't* say anything.

"They did," Audrey said finally, firmly, into the silence. "And they would, you know. I promise you that. They would want you to live."

"I don't know how."

The words came out on their own, as though spoken by someone else, the agonized voice unrecognizable as his own.

And there it was, the question that faced him every minute of every day, the question he had yet to find an answer for.

How was he supposed to live in a world where his wife and children were dead?

Lisa, the woman who had meant more to him than any he'd ever known, who'd had an effect on him like no other ever had—except Audrey, he registered with a twinge. Audrey affected him on an almost molecular level like that.

Morgan and Megan, the two most miraculous creatures he'd ever laid eyes on in his entire life. He'd been there when they'd drawn their first breaths, held them when each of them were small enough to fit in both his hands put together.

How was he supposed to get through each day, how was he supposed to feel anything, how was he supposed to *breathe,* without them in this world?

How?

"Tell me about them."

He slowly raised his head to meet her eyes, the compassion in them almost painful to see. "Why?"

"Because I think you need to talk about them," she said simply. "You haven't, have you? Since they died?" His silence was answer enough. "I know what it's like. When my parents died, I didn't have anyone to talk to about them, when I needed to the most. Hal dropped me off at school where I didn't know anybody, away from him, away from my friends. There were counselors there, but they were strangers. I didn't know them. I didn't want to talk to them, even though I knew I wanted to talk to someone. So I didn't talk to anybody. And it was hard. And I think it's only making it harder for you. Besides, I don't know anything about them, and I'd like to. So tell me about them."

No, he hadn't talked to anybody about them. He couldn't. It hurt too much.

Unsure what to say, he looked down at his hands.

We're going to cross the street now. Hold Daddy's hand.

He didn't know where the words came from, but suddenly they were there, echoing from the back of his mind in another voice he almost didn't recognize as his own. They were immediately followed by a feeling, the sensation of a small hand, delicate little fingers sliding into his palm, unhesitating, infinitely trusting. He stared at his right hand. All he saw there was the leather glove covering the scars he didn't have to see to visualize. But he didn't feel the texture of the leather or the scars marring his flesh. He only felt the weight of a small hand in his, as though it were actually there, and along with it, the surge of protectiveness, of possessiveness, of pure love that had always shot through his chest at the contact.

He almost gasped, the air rushing from his lungs as though he'd been punched.

He'd forgotten. God, he'd forgotten what it had felt like, his little girls' hands in his, the way they would smile up at him, how happy they always were to see him. Somehow, in the wake of their deaths, he'd forgotten that.

He closed his hand, trying to hold on to the feeling, the memory. He didn't want to forget it, even as other memories soon followed, one after another, flooding his head.

He only realized he'd started speaking when he heard the sound of his own voice. "My girls—their names were Megan and Morgan. Their mother came up with the names. I admit I wasn't that crazy about them at first. It seemed a little too cute to give twin girls matching names like that, but she was set on them, said that was who they were. I figured she should have more say in what they were called than I did, so I didn't argue with her. And when they were born, it didn't take me long to see she was right. That's who they were. I guess she knew that from the start."

He remembered Lisa in the hospital, holding the newborn girls, happy, exhausted, looking more beautiful than ever. And the first time he'd seen her, across the room at an embassy party, and known immediately that she was a woman he had to talk to. And how strangely nervous he'd been, despite all the women he'd ever spoken to in his life. And how it had felt the first time he'd made her smile.

He knew he was still talking, could feel his lips moving and sounds emerging from his throat. But mostly he remembered, one thought, one image after another, each leading into the next, almost faster than he could process. He tried to cling to each one, tried to absorb the emotions attached to it, even as there was always another one to follow.

Audrey didn't say anything. She didn't have to. It was enough to have her there, listening to every word. And he knew she was doing just that. He could feel her unwavering attention on his face, feel her smile at every happy memory, her sympathy at every tender one.

The memories came, one after another, vivid and clear, as though they'd happened recently instead of years ago, as though unfolding for him anew.

And for the first time in years, he felt no pain as he remembered, only the joys, great and small, that he'd been lucky enough to experience and that he never wanted to lose again.

Chapter Eleven

Audrey had never been very good at falling asleep when she needed to, when she knew she had to be up early the next day. It was as though her subconscious, knowing how badly she needed the rest, was perversely determined to deny it to her. So it was no surprise that on this night, possibly the last night she would ever sleep again, sleep proved as elusive as ever.

She stared into the darkness overhead, having long since given up even trying to drift off. Jason hadn't had to remind her of the risks. She knew all too well how dangerous the plan was. She'd thought coming to Barrett's Mill had been entering enemy territory. That was nothing compared to this. They were delivering themselves right into the hands of the man who wanted them dead, with no guarantee they would walk back out.

If they did, their problems would be solved.

If they didn't…

Well, then they wouldn't have any problems anymore, either, would they?

She tried to push the thought away, but it was impossible, her stomach twisting in knots. Jason might not care about whether he lived or died—and despite the breakthrough they'd shared that evening, she wasn't sure if anything had changed on that front—but she knew without a doubt she wasn't ready to die.

There were so many things she still wanted to do, places she wanted to see, experiences she'd always dreamed of and had yet to have. She'd never been to Paris. She'd never climbed a mountain. Never had a family. Children. Someone she loved, someone who loved her. Was it really only a week ago that she imagined what it might be like after seeing how happy Jackie was—

Jackie's wedding, she suddenly remembered with a pang. She'd missed it.

She had no trouble picturing Jackie and Brian, her fiancé, as they must have looked. First standing at the altar, gazing into each other's eyes, Jackie probably crying, a few tears sliding down her cheeks even as she was smiling with pure joy. And then, after the minister declared them man and wife and they turned toward the assembled guests hand-in-hand, walking back down the aisle with matching smiles on their faces.

Someday, she thought wistfully, swallowing hard. She'd always thought it would happen for her someday.

It never had. She'd had relationships over the years of course, but nothing that had lasted very long, nothing that she'd truly minded ending. She knew she wasn't very good at getting close to and opening up to people, perhaps because she'd been used to being alone for so long. But even more than that, she'd never met anyone she really wanted to completely open up to. Never met anyone who felt *right*.

Until Jason.

The thought came out of nowhere, popping into her head without warning.

Her immediate impulse was to deny it. It would certainly be easier if she could.

But she couldn't.

It didn't matter how short a time she'd known him. It felt like so much longer. The way she responded to him was unlike anything she'd felt toward anyone before, that connection she'd never felt with another person and had started to think might not actually exist.

He was everything Hal had made him out to be and more. Smart and sharp and, yes, incredibly good-looking, but also decent and principled. He could have let her walk away that first day, could have let her die, but he hadn't, even when he hadn't wanted to get involved, even though she was a stranger. He really was that elusive thing Richard Bridges only pretended to be—an honorable man. The unexpected kindness he'd shown her last night told her he had a good heart, and of course she knew he was capable of great love. She still remembered the love in his eyes when he'd spoken about his wife and children. She wondered, just for a moment, what it would be like to have him look at her like that.

A foolish thought of course, because that wasn't going to happen. Despite his breakthrough earlier tonight, she doubted he was suddenly going to decide to move on with his life, even if they had all the time in the world.

Her lips twisted in a humorless smile. She'd finally

met someone who might actually be the one, but it was too late, and the man wasn't really available.

And now she might never have another chance, never know what that kind of love was like.

"What's wrong?"

His voice floated out of the darkness, startling her. As he had the night before, he'd given up the bed to her and was stretched out on the floor beside it. She lay stock-still, wondering why he'd asked.

Then she felt a tear slip down her cheek, and realized she must have sniffled without knowing it.

Mortified, she swallowed to clear any sogginess in her throat and spoke as calmly as possible. "Nothing. I'm fine."

Hearing the words, even she didn't believe them. She knew before she heard him do it that he was pushing himself up from the floor. She swiped at her cheeks just before he flipped on the bedside light.

"No, you're not," he said quietly. She forced herself to meet his eyes. He sat on the floor, leaning against the bedside table, looking over at her.

Before she could say anything, he continued, "Is this about tomorrow? You really don't have to go."

She shook her head. "Forget it. We've been over this. I'm going." She waved a hand. "It's not about that anyway."

He rose to his feet and sat on the edge of the bed. "Then what is it?" he said gently.

It was too awkward to be lying there with him looking down at her. Sitting up herself, she sighed. "Nothing really. Trust me, it's nothing you want to hear about."

"You listened to me talk this evening. The least I can do is return the favor."

Lowering her head, she smiled sadly. "I was just thinking about all the things I'd never done that I wish I had, and how I might never get the chance now."

"Nothing's going to happen to you," he said fiercely, leaning closer to look into her face. "I'm not going to let it."

She met his eyes, saw the determination in them, and knew he meant every word. It was a nice promise, one she knew better than to take to heart. Neither of them knew what was going to happen tomorrow. They could be caught and killed before they ever had a chance to speak with Bridges. They might not be able to convince him and he'd have them killed anyway. They might not have any more time beyond the moment when they entered that house, if they even got that far. All they had was tonight.

A surge of adrenaline rushed through her at the thought.

Time hadn't completely run out yet. They had tonight. These few precious hours to make the most of…

And in an instant, staring into his face, her heart suddenly pounding in her chest, she knew without a doubt that she didn't want to waste them.

Only then did it hit her just how close they were sitting. The warmth she was feeling against her skin was the heat of his body mere centimeters away. All she had to do was shift her thigh slightly and their bodies would be in contact, all she had to do was reach out her hand to touch him.

She saw the moment he realized it, too, his eyes

flaring slightly. Saw the flash of awareness, and was reassuringly reminded she wasn't the only one who felt the attraction between them. In a heartbeat, the air between them thickened, the tension palpable, the sensation racing along her nerve endings and making her skin tingle.

Her gaze stroked over his face, taking in every perfect inch, finally arriving at his mouth.

He started to pull away, those tantalizing lips nearly vanishing from view as he ducked his head. He cleared his throat, his discomfort clear. "We should get some sleep," he said, his voice rough.

She threw her hand out without thinking, and caught his arm before he could rise from the bed. The feeling of his warm skin, of the muscles beneath immediately tensing and reacting to her touch, sent a jolt of heat through her. He didn't look at her, keeping his gaze resolutely averted, but she could tell from the pulse beating beneath her fingers that he felt it just as much as she did.

"I'm not going to be able to sleep tonight," she said quietly. "I don't think you are either."

He sucked in a ragged breath. "This isn't a good idea," he said, the acknowledgment of what was on the verge of happening sending a thrill up her spine.

"I don't care if it's a good idea. Because I don't know what's going to happen tomorrow, and I don't want to be alone tonight."

He didn't say anything, didn't do anything, for the longest moment. She reached up and placed her free hand on his right cheek, not willing to let go of this moment, of this chance, of him, so easily. He closed his eyes briefly at her touch, then opened them as she turned his face to hers.

"This is it, Jason," she said, her voice soft but firm. "You don't have any more time to decide. We could die tomorrow. Whether we live or die could be completely out of our hands. So you have to decide right now how you want to spend the next several hours of your life, because they're all you're guaranteed to have left. Do you want to spend them lying there doing nothing, or do you want to spend them living?"

She stared into his eyes and waited, breathless, having no idea how he would respond, what his choice would be. Hoping against hope that he wouldn't deny what was between them. That he would grant her this moment, what she wanted—*needed*—more than anything.

Finally, just when she was beginning to think it would never happen, when frustration and disappointment and sadness were starting to rise within her, he leaned forward and pressed his mouth to hers.

There was no trace of hesitation in his kiss. The first brush of his lips against hers was almost immediately followed by another, then another, then more still. He took her mouth hungrily, eagerly, deepening the experience with each subsequent caress of his lips against hers. Her breathing instantly quickened, her heart pounded harder and harder as she struggled to match him stroke for stroke, tried to absorb each moment, each sensation, even as she desperately wanted more.

In the very back of her mind, she registered something brushing against her cheek. Almost as soon as it did, it was gone. Seconds later he tore his lips from hers. Her eyelids fluttered open in time for her to see him starting to pull away.

"I'm sorry," he murmured, his breathing as fast and shallow as hers. He bent his head, his shoulders heaving. Dazed, not understanding, she followed his gaze to where he was looking.

His hands were in his lap, clenched tightly into fists. In the dim light from the single lamp, she could see he wasn't wearing his gloves.

That was what she'd felt, she realized. He'd placed his hand on her cheek, then immediately withdrew it when he realized what he'd done, when his scarred palm and fingers had made contact with her skin.

It was the first time she'd felt his bare hands against her skin. The brief contact hadn't lasted long enough for her to notice anything different. She'd barely felt it at all. But she knew without a doubt that she wanted to. She wanted to feel those hands all over her body. The scars didn't matter.

Reaching forward, she took his right hand in both of hers and slowly peeled his fingers open. His startled gaze flew to hers. Smiling softly, she brought his hand to her face, pressing his scarred palm to the curve of her cheek as she stared deep into his eyes. His skin wasn't as rough as she might have thought and he seemed to believe. It didn't matter anyway. All she felt was a hand, Jason's hand. Jason's fingers. Jason's skin. This was how he felt. Nothing had ever felt better, because this was him.

She watched as his gaze softened, the uncertainty melting into tenderness. That look in his eyes sent her pulse spiking again. He slowly stroked the pad of his thumb over her skin, the touch achingly gentle. Then he leaned forward and kissed her again.

The kiss was different this time. Slower. Deeper. The same hunger was there, the same eagerness, but each caress lasted longer, as though he wanted to savor every last bit of it, every last bit of her. She responded in kind, relishing every moment. Their tongues met, tangled, sliding against one another in a deliciously erotic dance. She couldn't get enough of it, the taste of him, the feeling of their mouths, their lips, moving together.

And yet it wasn't enough. She smoothed her hands down his chest, felt the muscles and warm flesh beneath the T-shirt and immediately wanted to feel him. Her fingers reflexively moved lower. Catching the bottom of his shirt, she started to work it up over his belly. Almost simultaneously, he reached for hers, tugging it higher. A laugh bubbled up from her throat, even as she felt his body rumble with one of his own.

Breaking apart, they shed their clothes together, helping each other out of each obstructive garment, watching each other as every new bit of bare skin was revealed. She felt his unwavering attention on her body, the heat of his gaze washing over her, her breasts, her belly. She reveled in the sensation, her arousal growing both under the force of his unyielding focus and what she saw herself.

She never took her eyes off him. She couldn't. His body was as beautiful as she'd known it would be. He was long and lean, his chest firm, his belly flat and tight. Her gaze followed the faint trail of hair over his nipples, down over his abdomen, then lower. She instinctively reached for the waistband of his shorts. He was a step ahead, shoving out of them, removing his underwear with them, if he'd been wearing any at all. It hardly mattered. All that did was that he was finally bare, the full proof of his arousal there before her. She reached out and took him in her hand, felt the hot, hard length of him pulsing, straining, against her fingers.

With a low growl, he pulled her hand away, then lifted her gently and lowered her onto the mattress, stretching out beside her. Their mouths found each other, their hands eagerly exploring each other's bodies. She trailed her fingers over the broad line of his shoulders, his chest, the muscles of his arms, even as she reveled in the feeling of his hands on her breasts, her side, between her legs… A gasp caught in her throat as his fingers slid into the thatch of hair there, unerringly finding her folds. One probing finger teased her, tested her, no doubt discovering just how wet and ready she was.

Two could play that game. Her hand found him again, stroking gently, coaxing another gratifying moan from his throat. He withdrew his hand, and she nearly whimpered in frustration. Circling his arms around her, he rolled her over onto her back, the weight of him comfortably heavy on top of her.

Then he suddenly stopped, freezing above her. He peered down at her, a frustrated look on his face. "Wait. I don't have anything."

It took her a moment to realize what he meant. She was about to suggest they throw caution to the winds—after all, what was the point in worrying about that if they didn't even know if they were going to survive tomorrow?—when she suddenly remembered.

"I do."

Pushing him off her, she scrambled off the bed and crossed to her bag, rummaging in it until she found what she was looking for. The condoms had been passed out at Jackie's girls' night out as a gag. Audrey had taken a few as part of the joke, never expecting to actually need them.

She'd never been so grateful for a party favor in her life.

Once she had them in hand, she dropped the bag and moved back to the bed. "Now where were we?" she said with a grin.

To her delight, he matched her grin. The sight of that magnificent smile lighting his beautiful face sent both fresh heat and something that felt curiously like joy bubbling through her. He should always smile. It was a crime that he didn't always look just like that.

He was lying on his back, propping himself up on his elbows to watch her, not self-conscious in the least. The pose was incredibly sexy, emphasizing the long, lean lines of his body, his erection still jutting up insistently from the rest of his prone form, and she knew she wanted him to stay just like that. As she climbed back onto the bed, he started to push up, but she planted a hand on his chest to keep him where he was, then straddled his legs. Dropping most of the foil packets on the bed, she tore open the one remaining in her hand. Reaching forward, she slowly rolled the condom over him, watching his face the whole time. He wasn't smiling anymore, but the emotions flashing across his face were just as satisfying. The desire. The need. The strain that said he was barely holding on.

As soon as he was covered, she moved forward, holding herself up on her knees and positioning herself over him. Then, peering straight into his amazing eyes, she lowered herself onto him.

She'd intended to go slow, to savor every moment. He didn't give her the chance. He thrust his hips upward at the same moment, her wetness easing his invasion, until he was buried in her, stretching her, filling her completely. She threw her head back, her eyelids sinking shut, a nearly breathless moan easing from her lungs and filling her ears. For a long moment, they simply stayed like that, their bodies joined, locked in that perfect moment of completion.

She felt his hands on her hips and opened her eyes just as he leaned forward, holding her in place. When they were face-to-face, he slid his hands around her and pulled her tight against him. The soft hairs on his chest brushed against her already sensitive nipples, creating a delicious friction. She barely noticed as she peered straight into his eyes just inches away. What she saw there took her breath away as much as that instant of invasion had, of having him inside her.

There was desire, of course, more than she could ever remember seeing before in a man's eyes. But also tenderness, something so caring that everything inside her went completely still at the sight of it. And something else—wonder or amazement or something she couldn't quite identify and wasn't sure she wanted to. If she did, she might start to question what caused it, might read something more into that look in his eyes than was really there.

What would it be like to have him look at her like that?

Lost in that look, she barely registered one of his

hands moving away from her back until it suddenly appeared in front of her face. Using the tips of his fingers, he gently brushed away a lock of hair that had fallen in front of her face without her even realizing it, tucking it behind her ear with the utmost care, never once taking his eyes from hers. Then he leaned forward and caught her lips with his, kissing her slowly, tenderly. She wrapped her arms around his neck, threaded her fingers through his hair. His hands returned to her hips, and almost immediately he began to move his own, pulling back slowly, withdrawing halfway, then driving into her again. She rocked against him, drawing him in deeper, tightening her muscles around him.

He tore his mouth away, moving it to the curve of her jaw, then the soft curve of her throat. Clinging to his hair, holding him close, she threw her head back. His thrusts gained speed gradually, deliberately. It was all more than she could begin to absorb, the feeling of him moving inside her, of his mouth on her neck, on her breasts, on her nipple, drawing it against his teeth and sucking hard. The pressure built deep inside her, driving higher and higher, harder and harder along with his thrusts. She could only hang on, his shoulders tensing and shifting beneath her arms, his thrusts coming faster and harder, until her climax finally came, her entire body seeming to shatter under the force of it, giving way to nothing but pure sensation. He was right there with her, his release shuddering through her, his moan vibrating along her skin, proof enough that she was still whole. She clung to him, floating on waves of pleasure.

And through it all, he continued to hold her, her

breasts tight against his chest, so she could feel his heartbeat and hers racing as one.

Lost in the sensations overwhelming her, she forgot about what lay in store for them only hours from now, about everything that faced them, about everything that kept him from truly being hers.

None of it mattered. The only thing that did was this, being here with him, this moment, right now. Something remarkable, unlike anything she'd ever experienced before. Something she wanted to hold on to as long as she could.

This man. For as long as she could have him.

Chapter Twelve

It was time. Jason knew it. Just as he knew he wasn't ready to leave this moment.

He lay perfectly still, Audrey nestled against his side, his arm around her shoulder. He knew she was awake, but she didn't say anything. Ever since they'd finally untangled their bodies and fallen back against the mattress, they'd simply lain there in a haze of comfortable silence, neither saying a word.

He should say something to her. The urge was there, deep down inside him, compelling him to speak. To comment on what had just happened between them. To acknowledge the significance. To admit that something had changed.

And it had. He couldn't even begin to deny it. He wasn't sure he wanted to. He just didn't know what it was that had changed, or maybe he just wasn't ready to admit it.

Too many thoughts, impressions, memories, were rushing through his head, too many emotions churning inside him. He couldn't begin to absorb them all, couldn't start to figure out what to say.

He didn't know what he could, didn't want to offer promises he wasn't sure he could keep.

There was only one thing he could bring himself to say, something he had to, something he didn't want to.

"Audrey?"

He felt her tense, the reaction sending a twinge of sadness through him. "Yes?"

"It's time to go."

If she felt any disappointment that their brief moment was over or that that was all he'd had to say, she didn't show it. She simply nodded and pushed away from him. He instantly felt the loss of her closeness.

He didn't let himself linger on it, pushing the feeling away and rolling over to the other side of the bed.

He didn't know what the experience they'd just shared really meant. He didn't know how much it truly changed, how much he was willing to let it. There were too many other things he had to focus on now. In the end, it might not even matter.

He didn't know if he was ready or in any way able to live.

All he could do was make sure that she did.

THE TUNNEL WAS EXACTLY as Marybeth had described it to them, a long, narrow passageway carved into the earth that was just wide enough for two people to walk side-by-side. Audrey still followed behind Jason, glancing back every once in a while and shining her flashlight into the darkness to keep an eye out behind them. They'd managed to break the padlock securing the entrance with a pair of bolt cutters, opening the door with little difficulty. Jason hadn't spotted any signs of a remote alarm that would tell someone the entry had been breached, but that didn't mean there wasn't one, or that a security guard wouldn't come along to check and notice the lock had been cut, the brush pushed away from the door. Just as they couldn't guarantee there wouldn't be someone waiting for them at the other end.

All they could do was continue with the plan, keep moving forward, and remain as alert as possible.

The passage was dry and cool. The only light came from their flashlights, narrowing their world to only what they could see in the beams. It was a disorienting feeling, and it began to seem as though they'd been walking forever, even though Audrey knew it should only take them a half hour at most to reach the house.

They moved in silence. It made sense to try to make as little noise as possible, neither of them knowing for sure what lay at the end of the tunnel or how far the sound would carry. But then, they really hadn't spoken at all since they'd left the inn. They'd driven to the tunnel in silence. Neither of them had said a word about what had happened only a few hours ago. It was probably better that way. No point making a big deal about it or turning it into something it wasn't. It wouldn't have even happened if it wasn't for their current circumstances. They were both better off focusing on those anyway.

The knowledge didn't prevent the urge to reach out and touch him, to feel him again.

She tried to tell herself it was simply because she didn't want to lose him, only to recognize the thought was probably far more accurate than she would have liked.

Finally, the tunnel arrived at a set of wooden steps leading upward. They must have reached the house.

At the top of the steps was a short landing. There were two wooden doors, one leading directly ahead, one to the right. Audrey knew they should be in the rear right corner of the house, with the doors corresponding to the two largest bedrooms on the second floor. Now that she'd seen it for herself, Audrey couldn't help but admire the ingeniousness of it. Marybeth had said the openings didn't appear to be doors on the other side. The walls themselves opened, the panels that released them discreetly hidden. It really was a perfect way into and out of the house without anyone knowing. Then again, maybe she shouldn't be surprised, given what she knew of the present-day Bridgeses. Deviousness was evidently a long-standing family trait.

According to Marybeth, the door straight ahead led to the master bedroom, Dick's room. The one to the right led to the room that had been Rich's. They had to hope it still was. Marybeth said it was the second largest bedroom in the house, so it seemed reasonable that he would have kept it, rather than move to a smaller one.

Stepping to the door on the right, Jason reached for the latch set flush in the wood. Once he had it in hand, he glanced back at her. Their eyes met, his uncertainty clearly mirroring her own. This was it.

She nodded once, urging him to proceed. He returned the nod, then turned the latch.

There was a small click as it released, then he slowly pushed the door in slightly.

They both listened intently. The soft sounds of a TV, its volume turned so low it was almost inaudible, reached them. Audrey didn't hear anything else—no voices, no movement.

Jason gently eased the door open farther, his body tense with alertness. Audrey waited for an alarm, even the slightest indication the motion had been detected.

Nothing. All remained calm and mostly silent in the room.

As the gap widened, Audrey caught a glimpse of what lay on the other side over Jason's shoulder. It was a bedroom, exactly as Marybeth had said. She saw curtains, a chair.

Finally, the gap was large enough for them to fit through. Jason slowly pushed his head around the corner. Evidently finding nothing, he straightened, then stepped through.

Moving on the tips of her toes, Audrey waited only a few seconds before following.

The room was large and spacious, more of a suite than a bedroom. The Bridges homestead might be called a farm, but Audrey should have known the house wouldn't be a simple farmhouse. The room was empty, although the fact that the TV and all the lights were turned on gave the impression that someone was here. It had to be a little after seven o'clock. Audrey quickly checked the exits. One opening led to what appeared to be an outer chamber, another to a bathroom.

Then she heard voices coming from another opening to the left.

Five seconds later, Rich and Julia Bridges stepped into the room.

Jason and Audrey both froze.

Rich was tying his tie, already dressed in a crisp

white shirt and dress slacks. He looked exactly as he did in all the pictures Audrey had studied, albeit a little smaller, as larger-than-life people tended to when seen in person. He was still a powerful figure, as handsome and magnetic in real life as he was in front of the cameras.

Her eyes on Rich, Audrey barely noticed Julia, until she stopped abruptly. As though reacting to his wife, Rich suddenly turned and spotted them, his eyes widening.

Jason instantly raised a hand in a warning gesture. "Before you call for security, Senator, you're going to want to hear us out. We're not here to hurt you. We just want to talk to you and try to come to an understanding so you will stop trying to hurt us."

"Hurt you? Who the hell are you?"

"My name is Jason Stone. This is Audrey Ellison. I'm sure you know who we are, since you've had someone trying to kill us for the past four days."

"I have no idea what you're talking about."

"Then I guess you also have no idea that Audrey's uncle was Hal Talmadge, who was working on a book about you, one that he believed would make headlines with what he had to reveal about you."

Tellingly, Bridges hesitated, his eyes flaring with surprise and darting in Audrey's direction.

"What exactly did he believe he had to reveal?"

"I'll get to that in a moment," Jason said. "But you should know that we've left that information with a third party who will release it if anything happens to us here today."

"All right," Bridges said slowly. "I understand. And I can promise you you're in no danger here."

"I appreciate that. And to guarantee that fact, I'm going to ask that your wife remain in the room."

Bridges glanced at his wife, finally noticing that she'd begun to move toward the door. At his nod, she stopped, remaining where she was.

He turned back to Jason. "Now why don't you tell me what it is you believe you know about me?"

"Gladly. Audrey?"

Audrey barely heard him, any more than she'd heard anything that had been said since Bridges had entered the room. She could only stare helplessly at the man, her mind trying to make sense of what she was seeing. Because his weren't the warm brown eyes she'd seen staring back at her from his campaign posters and all the photographs she'd studied, nor those of Will Kent, which she'd thought had been the same as his father's.

No, this man's eyes were blue, a startling, clear, light blue, the color unmistakable.

Contact lenses, she registered faintly. He must normally wear colored contact lenses. She and Jason must have intruded before he could put them in.

But why would he wear them? There was nothing wrong with having blue eyes. And yet, he wanted people to think he had brown eyes.

Like his father, Dick Bridges, did. Like his son, Will Kent, did.

An uneasy feeling slid through her system as something she'd learned in grade school, one of the most elementary rules of genetics, suddenly rose to mind.

Two blue-eyed parents couldn't make a brown-eyed child. Yet Will Kent had brown eyes. Marybeth was obviously his mother and Audrey was certain she had blue eyes. But this man also had blue eyes. Marybeth had no reason to lie about Bridges being Will's father, which meant he had to be. So the only possible explanation was—

"You're not Richard Bridges."

The words came out on their own, muted with the shock jolting through her, but she didn't regret them. Instead, a sense of certainty fell over her once she spoke the words aloud.

And she knew she was right.

"What are you talking about?" the man before her asked, but she caught the hint of alarm in those clear blue eyes.

If he wasn't Rich Bridges, then logic said there was only one person he could be, one solution that tied up all the pieces they'd accumulated over the past several days.

She arched a brow. "Tim Raymer, I presume?"

Ever the politician, he didn't let his expression betray him. He frowned, his eyebrows drawing together in a display of confusion she would have believed if she hadn't known any better. "I don't understand. What are you talking about?"

"Audrey?" Jason asked, his confusion obvious in his voice.

"Rich Bridges had brown eyes," she explained without shifting her focus from Raymer. "Look at him. This man's eyes are blue. I guess we caught you before you could put your contacts in," she told Raymer.

He choked out a laugh. "This is preposterous. So I wear contact lenses. That doesn't mean I'm someone else, whoever it is you think I am."

"Tim Raymer," Audrey repeated. "The high school sweetheart of Julie Ann Foster, who just happened to go on to marry Rich Bridges a year after Raymer's death. Everyone we talked to seemed to think that must have meant she was two-timing Tim, dating Rich at the same time the summer before he left for Europe." She glanced at Julia Bridges, who stood frozen, her eyes round. "But you weren't, were you? You weren't dating Rich at all. You were dating Tim the whole time." She looked back at the supposed Rich Bridges. "It was Tim who went to Europe. Tim, who came back and married Julie Ann Foster. Which means it must have been Rich whose burned body was found in Tim Raymer's truck." Poor Marybeth, she thought with a twinge. Rich hadn't left her at all.

Neither Julia nor her husband said anything. They simply stared at her.

Bridges/Raymer finally cleared his throat. "And this is what you believe you know?"

"No," Audrey admitted. "That was something else. I didn't know this until just now when I saw your eyes. Because, like I said, Rich Bridges—the *real* Rich Bridges—had brown eyes. I'm sure there are plenty of people who remember that."

"You can't prove any of this," he said calmly.

Audrey thought quickly. She didn't want to drag Marybeth and Will into this if she didn't have to. Then again, maybe she didn't have to.

"Perhaps not," she agreed easily. "But I can prove enough to make things messy and raise some uncomfortable questions for you. Like Jason told you, we have information waiting to be released if anything happens to us here. As you can probably guess from what I just said, we've been looking into the accident in which Tim Raymer supposedly died. So did my uncle. He spoke with the medical examiner who performed the autopsy on the body discovered in Tim Raymer's truck. I'm sure you know what he found."

He looked almost bored, though his gaze never wavered. "Do I?"

This was where it got tricky. "The ME found injuries on the body that were inconsistent with a car accident," she guessed, putting together what must have happened based on what they knew. "The victim was dead before the car crashed and caught fire. The ME covered it up on Dick's orders, but he retained a copy of the file in case he one day had a chance to tell the truth. He didn't know about the switch. He thought it was Tim Raymer who died, Tim Raymer whose murder was covered up. He gave a copy of those records to my uncle, who digitized them. I have a copy." She drew the scenario to its logical conclusion, her unwavering voice never revealing that she had no proof at all. Then she continued, "Now, combine those records with the fact that Rich Bridges left town immediately after Tim Raymer's death, spent the next year on an out-of-character trip in Europe, then returned to Barrett's Mill and married Tim Raymer's girlfriend shortly thereafter. I think people will start to question what happened to Tim, why Dick ordered the ME to call it an accident when it wasn't, and why Rich suddenly left for Europe, only to marry Tim's girlfriend upon his return. They probably won't guess the truth—too outlandish, too unbelievable, of course. Instead, it'll seem like Rich probably killed Tim." The conclusion they, and most likely Hal, had drawn.

Audrey shrugged lightly. "I may not be able to prove you're Tim Raymer, but you might start finding it a lot more difficult to be Rich Bridges."

Finished, she held his gaze and waited to see how he would respond.

At first he didn't, simply studying her steadily through those foreign blue eyes.

Julia finally stepped forward into the silence. "This is ridiculous," she said. "I'm getting security."

"Don't," Tim said before Audrey or Jason could. His shoulders sagged as though bearing the weight of the world. "What do you want?" he asked them.

"I told you," Jason said. "I want some assurance that you and your people will stop trying to kill us."

"And I told you I have no idea what you're talking about."

"You also told Ms. Ellison that what she's saying is ridiculous and you're not Tim Raymer, and I think we've moved beyond that. Why don't we stop wasting time and be straight with each other?"

"I'm telling you the truth," Tim said impatiently, raking a hand through his perfect hair. "I most certainly have not been trying to kill anybody. I would never do something like that."

Audrey wouldn't have thought it possible, but she believed him. He really had no idea what they were talking about. She stared at him, stunned. But if not him...

She glanced at Julia, who appeared equally bewildered. Then that left...

"What about Dick Bridges?" Audrey asked.

Tim narrowed his eyes on her face. "What about him?"

"Is it something he would do?"

He shook his head. "No, of course n—" He cut off, his defense of Dick coming to an abrupt end, uncertainty flashing across his features.

"Obviously, Dick Bridges must have been involved from the beginning for this to have happened," Audrey pointed out. "Did you and he conspire to kill Rich so you could take his place?"

"Don't be ridiculous. Nobody killed Rich Bridges. He killed himself."

Audrey exhaled sharply. "Oh, come on."

"It's true," Julia said, a quiver in her voice. "I was there when Dick showed him the body."

"He hanged himself in the barn," Tim said. "Dick called me at home and asked me to come right away. Julie was with me, though he didn't know that. I told her to stay in the car, but she didn't. Dick showed me Rich's body. He'd already cut it down. Dick said they'd argued about Rich's future. Rich didn't want to go college, he didn't want to do any of the things Dick wanted him to. Apparently, Dick was pretty rough on him, threatened to cut him off unless Rich did exactly what he wanted to. Rich ended up storming out. Dick didn't hear him drive off, so when Rich didn't come back within a few hours, Dick went looking for him. That's when he found him like that in the barn. He was already dead. He must have snapped, finally had enough of all the pressure. That's when Dick called me."

"He wanted you to help him cover it up?"

"And to make me an offer."

"To take Rich's place," Audrey concluded.

"I thought he was crazy. I'm sure it still sounds that way. He said Rich was his legacy, and he couldn't bear the thought of his legacy dying like that. Rich and I were roughly the same height, the same age. He knew I was smart, ambitious, a hard worker. So he laid out this plan whereby we'd burn the body in my car and make it seem like I had died. Meanwhile, he would send me to Switzerland, to a clinic he knew with the best, most discreet plastic surgeons in the world. They would give me a new face, turn me into Rich Bridges." He shook his head. "I really didn't think they would be able to pull it off, but they did."

"Why would you agree to go along with that?" she asked.

He looked at her in disbelief. "Why wouldn't I? I had a miserable life. My only family was an uncle who couldn't stand me any more than I could him. I was going to have to work my tail off to pay for college. Dick was offering me everything. A new life, a top education, a name that means something in this world. He was opening every door I never would have had a chance to approach. I could do things as Rich Bridges. I *have* done things. Do you think Tim Raymer would be standing here today? Would anyone in this town, let alone this country, be so eager to vote for Tim Raymer for president?"

"What about Rich Bridges? Did he deserve to have his identity stolen, his life forgotten so easily?"

"Why should I worry about his life, when he thought so little of it? He killed himself. The spoiled brat had every advantage in the world, every opportunity handed to him, and he didn't even appreciate it. He just threw it all away."

"No, he didn't," Audrey said firmly. "Rich Bridges wouldn't have killed himself. There's no way."

"I'm telling you he did."

"I saw it myself," Julia said.

"No," Audrey repeated. "You saw a dead body. And you," she said to Raymer, "told me Dick showed you the body. Neither of you saw Rich kill himself. From the sound of it, you didn't even see him hanging. You said Dick had already cut the body down. Except, I would be surprised if it was ever hanging in the first place. If it was, it only would have been for show, to make sure the bruising on the neck was convincing. Because if you didn't help Dick Bridges kill his son—and I believe you didn't—then Dick must have done it himself. It's the only explanation."

"That's ridiculous. Why would Dick kill his own son?"

Audrey had no trouble picturing what had happened, what Dick's reaction must have been when Rich had told him he didn't intend to start college that fall. "Like you said, he didn't appreciate what he had. He wanted to walk away from it all, everything Dick wanted him to do. And when Dick realized that this time he wasn't going to be able to force Rich to obey, he must have lashed out. The only question is whether it was in the heat of the moment or deliberate."

"You have no way of knowing that."

"Yes, I do."

"That's enough."

The voice came from the opening to the tunnel behind them. Audrey recognized it as soon as she heard it. She jerked her head to the speaker.

Dick Bridges stepped into the room, the opening to his own room visible behind him. He was staring at her, hatred burning in his eyes. Audrey barely noticed, her attention focused on the object he held in his right hand.

It was a gun equipped with a silencer.

And it was pointed right at her.

Chapter Thirteen

Jason took one look at the gun in Dick Bridges's hand and it was all he could do not to dive in front of Audrey. Only the sight of Bridges's finger on the trigger and the knowledge that any sudden movement might set the man off held him in place.

"What are you doing?" Tim Raymer said, finally breaking the silence that had fallen over the room in the wake of Dick Bridges's sudden appearance.

Dick didn't so much as glance in his direction, never taking his eyes off Audrey. "Dealing with a situation."

With the bastard's attention off him, Jason slowly started to shift in her direction. If he could just move in front of her and block her with his body...

"It was you all along," Audrey said bluntly. "You had my uncle killed. You had that man try to kill us, too."

"You're just full of answers today, aren't you, Ms. Ellison?" Dick said dispassionately. "Don't move, Mr. Stone. One more inch and I won't hesitate to shoot."

Dick didn't even glance at him as he said it. Jason forced himself to stop when it was the last thing he wanted to do. "Let's all calm down, sir. There's no reason why anyone has to be shot."

"I believe Ms. Ellison spent the past several minutes eloquently laying out the reasons you both need to be shot."

"You can't be saying this is true," Tim said, his tone incredulous. "You've been trying to kill them? You killed Rich?"

"It's like you said, he didn't appreciate who he was, the opportunities I'd provided him. He wanted to throw it all away."

"Did he tell you why?" Audrey asked.

"He said he was going to live his own life," Dick scoffed. "The life he wanted. He was going to be *happy*."

So that was it, the reason people as politically savvy as the Bridgeses were willing to launch a presidential campaign despite a secret as explosive as an abandoned illegitimate child out there like a time bomb. Because none of them knew. Rich hadn't told his father about Marybeth and the baby. Was it because he hadn't had a chance, or because he'd been trying to protect them from Dick Bridges's rage, the same rage the man must have directed at him? Even now, just recalling the moment, Dick's anger was palpable.

"So you killed him," Tim concluded, his voice still ringing with disbelief.

"It was an accident," Dick said with no discernable emotion. "We argued. He tried to walk away from me. I grabbed his arm and we struggled. He fell, hit his head. I tried to wake him up, but it was clear he was dead."

"And you immediately came up with a backup plan to preserve your legacy," Audrey said.

"I wasn't going to let Rich ruin everything I'd planned

for his life." He looked at Tim. "I'd been watching you for a long time. I knew how smart you were, how driven, what a hard worker you were. I knew you were more worthy of my name than he was. And then came the moment when I knew I could make that the case."

If Tim was at all flattered by the man's words, he gave no indication.

"Just like you weren't going to let my uncle ruin everything when he found out too much about the supposed death of Tim Raymer," Audrey said.

"He didn't know the whole truth." Dick sniffed. "But he certainly knew far more than he had any business knowing. Just like you do."

With that, Dick refocused the gun directly on Audrey's chest, the sight sending Jason's adrenaline surging. He didn't have the slightest doubt the man intended to pull the trigger. He just didn't know if he had a chance of getting in front of her in time.

"No," Tim said, stepping forward. "You're not shooting anyone."

"Don't be absurd," Dick scoffed. "They'll ruin everything!"

"There's nothing to ruin." Tim raised his chin, cold resolve settling over his features. "I'm going out there and announcing that I've decided I'm not running for president after all."

Dick stared at him, his expression rapidly turning to horror. "What are you saying?"

"I'm not doing this. I've been thinking a great deal over the past few days about everything we've done, and having doubts about whether I can actually go through with trying to convince the American people to make me their president while lying to them about who I am. Can you imagine what would happen if I did win, and then the truth came out, the way it would shake this country? Not to mention my children. And that was before I knew everything you'd done. My God, you killed your own son!"

"It was an accident!"

"Having Hal Talmadge killed wasn't! Trying to have Mr. Stone and Ms. Ellison killed wasn't!"

"These were necessary measures. They've involved themselves in something that is none of their business."

"This is politics. Having someone killed is never a 'necessary measure.' I can't be a party to that. I won't."

Jason listened to what he was saying with a sense of awe. Raymer's words sounded just as passionate as any speech he'd ever given as Rich Bridges. It suddenly struck him that his instinct about this man hadn't been wrong, nor had any of the people who would have voted for him.

He really was a good man, even if he wasn't the man everyone thought he was.

Jason glanced over at Julia Bridges to see how she was reacting. It was her ambitions he was throwing away as well.

To his surprise, her eyes brimmed with tears, an expression of unmistakable pride on her face. And he knew that, however their marriage had come to be, this woman really did love her husband.

"You can't do this!" Dick said. "Not after everything I've done for you!"

"Don't pretend your actions were some great act of charity. Everything you've done was for yourself."

"I gave you my name!"

"The name you denied me in the first place!"

A stunned silence hung over the room in the wake of Raymer's outburst. Dick glared at the man, his jaw clenched tightly. And there it was—one last piece of the puzzle. Dick Bridges was Tim Raymer's unnamed father. It made a certain amount of sense—why Dick had thought of him to replace Rich, how they'd been able to pull off the masquerade. Plastic surgery alone couldn't make someone look exactly like someone else. But someone who was related, a half brother with similar bone structure—perhaps? That would make it a lot easier.

Dick abruptly swung the gun toward Raymer and aimed it at the younger man's chest. "I wouldn't let Rich throw everything away. I'll be damned if I'll let you do it, either!"

The surprise that briefly flared across Tim's face quickly faded. He lifted his chin slightly and met Dick's eyes, his expression composed, as though completely unfazed by the gun pointed at him. "What are you going to do, Dick? Shoot me? Do you really think you'll get away with that? How will you explain it?"

"An assassination." He jerked his head toward Jason and Audrey. "These two broke in and killed you. I managed to catch them in the act and killed them, but it was too late to save you. Maybe I'll run in your stead. I'm sure people will be much more sympathetic to a grieving father."

An eerie calm fell over Jason. It was a crazy plan, but

Dick Bridges had already pulled off one crazy plan in the replacement of his son. Was there a chance in hell he could get away with this, too?

He couldn't begin to calculate the likelihood and probabilities. Because a heartbeat later, Dick swung the gun and aimed it directly at him.

Jason froze, his mind going blank. As he stared down the barrel of the gun, the implications truly hit him for the first time, the knowledge that they could all be about to die.

And in a flash of insight so definite there was no doubting it, he knew.

He wasn't ready to die.

The need pounded through him, rushing through his veins, filling his head, a primal instinct that was undeniable.

He wanted to live.

Jason glanced at Audrey. She stared at Dick, her head held high, no fear in her eyes.

Respect welled up inside him. God, she was amazing. Next to dying, the last thing he wanted to do was let her go.

"And what about Julia?" Tim asked Dick with deadly calm. "Are you going to kill her, too?"

Dick shot a glare at the woman, his hatred obvious. "I should have done it a long time ago, the minute she blackmailed you into marrying her. If I'd known she was there that night, that she'd overheard everything, it would have been done then."

"It'll never work, Dick. You only have one gun. Even if it's not registered in your name, do you really think anyone will believe they killed the two of us, then you managed to come in and get the gun away from them and kill them?"

Jason could see the man thinking quickly, but he didn't say a word, obviously not having a response to that.

Tim simply shook his head. "It's over, Dick."

The older man's face darkened with rage. "I'm not going to stand by and watch you throw away everything I've worked for!"

Tim eyed him coolly. "I'm afraid you don't have a choice."

Dick stared at him for a long moment. Then his gaze suddenly went cold, the corners of his mouth lifting in a faint smile. "I would have thought you'd have learned a long time ago. We all have choices."

Jason's pulse leaped in alarm. Bridges was going to do something. Jason braced himself, ready to launch himself in front of Audrey at the slightest indication the gun was going to move back toward her.

He didn't get the chance.

Before anyone could react, Dick raised the gun to his temple and pulled the trigger.

Jason saw it unfold in vivid detail. The explosion of blood. The way Dick's body jerked. The life snuffing out of his eyes. And the slow collapse of his body as it crumpled to the floor.

At first, Jason could only stare at the body in shock. He finally managed to raise his eyes and look at Audrey. She appeared just as stunned, her eyes dazed as she peered down at the man.

The silence stretched on, no one moving, until Raymer finally lifted his head and looked at Audrey.

He cleared his throat softly. "I know I have no right to ask this of you, but for the sake of my wife and children, I'm going to do it anyway," he said sadly. "I would be grateful if you wouldn't reveal what was discussed here to anyone. I'm very sorry for what happened to your uncle and for everything you've gone through. But no good can come of the truth being revealed. Dick's been punished, and I meant what I said. I'm going to announce I'm not running after all, and that I'll be retiring from the senate. I'm sure everyone will believe Dick's suicide was a result of my telling him that. I don't really care what happens to me, but my wife and children are innocent in this. They don't deserve to be hurt by this."

At first Jason could only stare in disbelief. To think that they would be a part to covering up the truth after everything that had been done…

But of course, Raymer hadn't done any of this, Jason acknowledged. Neither had his wife or children. Yet they would be the ones hurt if the whole truth was revealed. Remembering how Audrey hadn't wanted to reveal the truth about Will Kent's paternity to prevent him and his mother from being hurt, he knew what her answer would be before she gave it.

She glanced at him, a question in her eyes. Jason gave one small nod, agreeing with what he already knew she'd decided.

Audrey turned her attention back to Raymer. "We won't tell."

The man exhaled deeply. "Thank you."

"But if anything happens to us, you can be assured

we'll leave arrangements for the truth to come out," Jason said.

Raymer simply nodded at him. "I understand. No one connected with me will pose a threat to you, and I will make sure anyone else Dick may have hired to do his dirty work is called off."

Jason studied him, finally deciding he believed him. "All right."

"Good," Raymer said. "Please leave the same way you came. I don't know how to explain your presence here, and I'd rather not have to try."

Jason nodded tightly and turned to Audrey. She was already in motion, starting for the still-open door. They didn't speak, quickly moving to the passage. When they reached it, he guided Audrey into the opening first, then glanced back before following.

Tim Raymer stood staring down at Dick Bridges's body. Julia moved to her husband's side and gently placed her hand on his arm. After a moment, he reached up and placed his hand over hers.

The sight of them there, standing together, struck a chord within him. Everything they'd worked for was in tatters, but somehow he knew they would be okay. They still had each other. They would move on.

Sometimes, it was all a person could do.

Lowering his eyes, Jason finally followed Audrey into the passageway and pulled the door shut behind them.

Chapter Fourteen

Audrey stepped out of the inn and came to a stop on the front porch, wincing at the brightness of the midday sun. So much had happened today, it seemed as though it should be later. It was hard to believe it was only a little after noon.

There were plenty of hours left in the day, yet it felt like she'd run out of time.

She gazed down toward the car. Jason was waiting for her in it, having decided to let her have her last conversation with Marybeth in private. Now that that was done, all Audrey had to do was walk down there and join him. Within minutes they would be on their way out of town. By the end of the day she would be home, a place it had seemed like she would never see again. She could go back to her life, her job, her friends.

She should be happy. Glad. Relieved. The ordeal was over. And she was glad for that.

But she wasn't ready for everything to be over, especially something that had barely just begun.

She wasn't the only one who would be returning to a life, even if Jason's wasn't much of one. She pictured him as she'd first discovered him, in that dingy bar, the thought making her heart squeeze. She supposed he would want to get back to that, to a life of nothing, unbothered by the rest of the world. The notion was painful to consider. But she couldn't make him want to live. He had to make that choice for himself. She'd spent too much of her life hoping for a relationship with someone who couldn't bring himself to reciprocate. She couldn't do it again.

Drawing a breath, she forced her feet into motion and moved down the front steps.

He was sitting in the driver's seat, staring straight ahead, his expression as stoic as ever. Her heart stuttered at the sight of his profile. She kept her eyes on his face as she approached, wanting to take it in as long as she could, especially while he didn't know.

All too soon, she reached the car. As she pulled the door open, the sounds of voices reached her. Jason glanced over, then leaned forward and turned off the radio.

"Anything new?" she asked, sliding into the passenger seat. By the time they'd left the Bridgeses' estate and made it back to the car, the airwaves had been full of reports of an ambulance being summoned to the house, and speculation about what it might mean. Just as they made it back to the inn, word had come that "Rich" would be addressing reporters shortly, long before the event scheduled to take place that afternoon.

"Bridges finally made his statement," Jason confirmed. "It's like he told us. He announced that he's decided not to run for president after all, and that he's retiring from the senate as well. He said it was a personal decision for the sake of his family. He also said that Dick had died suddenly this morning, but didn't mention how. He didn't take any questions."

"I'm sure that has led to plenty of speculation."

"It's all anyone's talking about on every station. So far, everyone just seems baffled, as you'd expect. I imagine it'll only get worse when they find out how Dick died."

"Do you really think they'll admit that Dick killed himself, or will they try to cover it up?"

"Raymer didn't seem like he felt like covering up anything for Dick anymore," he pointed out.

"Just for himself and his family."

He glanced at her. "You sure you're okay with the full truth not coming out?"

"I am," she said without hesitation. "I know how much the book meant to Hal, but it looks like he didn't even uncover the whole story. The people responsible for his death and those of the others have been punished. Having the truth come out now would just hurt people who don't deserve it."

In the end, she'd decided there was only one person who really needed to know the truth. Marybeth Kent had wept when Audrey told her what happened to the real Rich Bridges. There had been a great deal of sadness in her tears, but Audrey sensed a bit of relief, as well, at the knowledge that Rich hadn't abandoned her and their child. She hadn't read him wrong. He *had* loved her.

"Are you going to tell Will?" Audrey had asked her.

Marybeth had appeared to consider the question for a long moment before slowly shaking her head. "I don't know," she said. Audrey had believed that the woman honestly didn't know in that instant, but she also suspected Marybeth would ultimately decide not to. Will Kent had his own burgeoning political career to consider. The last thing he needed was to be connected with the ugliness surrounding Dick Bridges.

Thinking of Marybeth, Audrey gave one last glance at the inn. Regardless of the reasons that had brought her here, she knew she would have fond memories of the place, if only because of one particular night she'd spent within its walls.

A lump rose in her throat, and she quickly swallowed it, not about to linger on the emotion. She turned back to find Jason studying her, his eyes unreadable. She resisted the urge to squirm self-consciously in her seat. "Ready to go?" she asked.

"Yeah," he said softly. "I'm just trying to figure out where to go."

"You don't have to take me to Baltimore, if that's what you're worried about. I should probably go back to D.C. and see if I can track down my car. I'm not holding my breath that it hasn't been stolen, but maybe there's a chance it's only been towed. If I can't find it, I can take the train back."

"And if I do want to take you back to Baltimore?"

Everything inside her went still. "Why would you want to do that?"

A hint of uncertainty entered his eyes just before he glanced away, facing forward again. "I've been sitting here thinking about my shabby apartment, and that neighborhood, and the bar. All the places that pretty much became my world over the past few years. I never really thought about them before, never bothered because I didn't care. And now that I do, I keep thinking how sad those places are. It's really no way to live, is it?"

"No, it's not."

"I guess I'm in no hurry to get back there. I don't really want to go back to that—to any of that." He finally looked at her again, his eyes intent and burning with so much naked emotion her heart leaped. "But most of all, I don't want to say goodbye to you."

"Then don't," she said automatically, the words coming out on their own.

"And you'd be okay with that?"

"Yes," she said, the voice that emerged from her throat hoarse with feeling. "I don't want to say goodbye to you, either."

He looked at her steadily, unwaveringly, and she watched the rush of emotions washing over his face, hope and tenderness and relief and joy and so much more than she could begin to absorb, all igniting the same within her. The shadows in his eyes weren't gone, not completely, but they'd begun to fade, and his gaze was filled with so much more.

Then slowly, finally, he smiled.

At the sight of that smile, her heart pounded faster. The reaction was more than just a response to how devastatingly handsome he looked with that smile on his lips. It was a response to what that smile meant. It said far more than his words ever could, and a sudden lightness filled her chest.

He looked alive, more so than she'd ever seen him.

He really was finally ready to live.

She matched his smile, happiness soaring through her. This wasn't the ending she'd expected after all.

It was a beginning.

"All right then," he said. "Let's go."

She didn't bother asking where they were going as he started the engine and shifted the car into gear. It didn't matter. They'd figure it out. All that mattered was that they were going together, off into a future that was theirs to find.

And as he pulled out of the driveway and they hit the road, Audrey leaned back in her seat, her smile deepening.

Hal had thought the book would be his legacy. It wouldn't, but he'd left one just the same.

Because of him, she and Jason had found each other. He'd brought them together. Their future had come about because of him.

And that was a pretty good legacy for anyone to leave.

* * * * *

Harlequin

INTRIGUE

COMING NEXT MONTH

Available April 12, 2011

REQUEST YOUR FREE BOOKS!
2 FREE NOVELS PLUS 2 FREE GIFTS!

Harlequin
INTRIGUE
BREATHTAKING ROMANTIC SUSPENSE

*Selene wanted nothing to do with the father of her son,
Alex; but Aristedes had other plans...that included them.*

*Read on for an sneak peek from
THE SARANTOS SECRET BABY by Olivia Gates,
available April 2011, only from Harlequin Desire.*

"You were right to turn my marriage offer down," Aristedes said.

And Selene found her voice at last, found the words that
would not betray the blow he'd dealt her. "Thanks for letting me know. You didn't have to come all the way here,
though. You could have just let it go. I left yesterday with
the understanding that this case is closed."

Before the hot needles behind her eyes could dissolve
into an unforgivable display of stupidity and weakness, she
began to close the door.

The door stopped against an immovable object. His flat palm.

"I can't accept that." His voice was low, leashed.

What did her tormentor mean now? Was he ending one
game only to start another?

She raised eyes as bruised as her self-respect to his,
found nothing there but solemnity and determination.

Before she could voice her confusion, he elaborated. "I
never let anything go unless I'm certain it's unworkable. I
realize I made you an unworkable offer, and that's why I'm
withdrawing it. I'm here to offer something else. A work-
ability study."

She leaned against the door, thankful for its support and
partial shield. "Your son and I are not a business venture
you can test for feasibility."

His gaze grew deeper, made her feel as if he was trying
to delve into her mind, take control of it. "It's actually the

other way around. I'm the one who would be tested."

She shook her head. "Why bother? I know—and *you* know—you're not workable. Not with me."

His spectacular eyebrows lowered over eyes she felt were emitting silver hypnosis. "You're right again. Neither you nor I have any reason to believe that isn't the truth. The only truth. It might be best for both you and Alex to never hear from me again, to forget I exist. But then again, maybe not. I'm only asking for the chance for both of us to find out for certain. You believe I'm unworkable in any personal relationship. I've lived my life based on that belief about myself. I never really had reason to question it. But I have one now. In fact, I have two."

Find out what happens in
THE SARANTOS SECRET BABY by Olivia Gates,
available April 2011, only from Harlequin Desire.

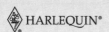